MUST

Danielle Barrios

This novel is a work of fiction. Names, characters, places and incidents are the product of the author's imagination or are used fictitiously. Any resemblance to actual events, locales, or persons, living or dead, is coincidental.

MUST LOVE COFFEE
Cover Design by Q Design
Edited by Lawrence Editing www.lawrenceediting.com
Final Proofing by: Lia Fairchild at Finishing Touch Editing.

ISBN-10:1983892270

BISAC: Fiction / Contemporary Women

Acknowledgements

I'd like to thank my alpha reader, my mother, Sharon Estes, for her various readings of multiple drafts, and to my beta readers, Amy Miles, Julie Cassar, Kari Suderley, Jenn Tenney, Angela Domenichelli, and Tim Pugliese for lending some male perspective.

Danielle Bannister

Dedication

This book is for my late aunt Jackie, whom I've named the character of Jackie Abbey after. You are missed but not forgotten.

Danielle Bannister

Chapter 1

MUST LOVE COFFEE. I frowned at the words on the screen. Those three words were the only ones I could think to list in my "wants" section of this stupid online dating site. For the last half hour, I'd been staring at the screen, trying to come up with something better. Apparently, having an addiction to caffeine was the only thing I wanted.

That wasn't totally true, but it's not like you can say, *I'm looking for someone with big tits and who's great in bed.* Women don't care for that. I had to be serious. I needed to list things that reflected who I was. What was I besides a coffee shop owner?

Therein was the problem. No chick in their right mind was going to love a balding, four-eyed guy in his mid-forties, who had no aspirations outside of waking up in the morning without a hangover.

Twenty years ago I could have bragged about my dreams of starting a band and traveling the world. But now, my guitar sat collecting dust in my perpetual bachelor pad. I was no longer the sort of guy a girl would be jumping up and down to meet, let alone date.

That's not to say I was this hideous creature from a horror movie. It's just, over the last ten years or so, I'd become...average—nothing to write home about. The sort of person you'd pass on the street and not even notice.

Somehow, I'd become an adult who couldn't even keep a house plant alive. A few years ago, that idea didn't faze me in the least. Staring down the barrel of middle age terrified me. I was going to die alone if something didn't change.

Hence the dating sites. I needed to branch out of my tiny town of Bucksville, New Hampshire. Because, as my sister, Jackie, had so eloquently put it: "You've slept with every woman in a ten-mile radius over the years. Online dating is your only option left."

That wasn't true. Well, not really. I hadn't slept with *all* the women in this town, just a dozen or so...several times over. That wasn't my fault, though. There weren't a lot of options in a small town.

Maybe that's what started this sudden mid-life panic. The old standby girls just weren't doing it for me anymore. I was craving...I don't know, something more.

"What's wrong with one-night stands, Finny, old boy?" my pal Joe had asked one night at the bar, wiggling his thick eyebrows. Joe had been my dad's best friend and was in the pub more often than in his day job, it seemed. His face was always red from drink, which stood out against a bad bleached-blond hair dye. It was a look that may have made him attractive back in the day, but now made his bloated face stand out like a stop sign.

I'd known Joe since I was a kid. After Dad passed, Joe sort of stepped in, thinking I needed a father figure. Or maybe he just wanted a drinking buddy. Dad had never been a big drinker, but I sure was after his death. Joe had seen some of my darkest days. He cleaned up my drunken messes more times than a friend should, I'm ashamed to admit.

"Finn, you're in the prime of your life," Joe had said the other night. "This is when you should be going out and buying a convertible, banging some college chick, or moving to Paris. It's not the time to settle down!"

Joe was talking out of his ass. He was happily married, and as far as I knew, as faithful as they came. Still, he was getting older and likely wanted to live vicariously through my bad life choices. And boy, oh boy, did I make a few of those.

"I gotta grow up sometime, Joe. I'm not in college anymore," I said, nursing the last of my beer.

College. Man, back then, there had been no shortage of women vying for a spot on my arm. All the sorority girls wanted to date the hunky grunge rocker who played free gigs at their parties. It didn't matter they didn't know my name or even what my major was. The truth was, I didn't care about theirs either.

After college I had plans—epic, backpacking through Europe plans—except, I didn't have the cash to do it. So, I'd decided I'd earn my way there by taking on a few shifts at my folks' shop, Must Love Coffee. A summer job. That turned into working just a few months after the season ended. Then, months turned into years, and all my grand aspirations of a better life outside of the snore-inducing Bucksville faded away, right along with my hairline.

Things were monotonous until Ma was killed by a drunk driver, and I went into a tailspin when Dad died of a heart attack three months later. From that point on, life pretty much sucked.

I was thirty-five when they passed. A full decade had slid through my fingers...and what had I done in that time? Other than keeping the shop open? Nothing. I hadn't even moved out of the stupid little apartment above the shop I'd had when I was in college. I had made no attempt to better my situation, so it was my own fault. And yet, I was still bitter with the universe that my life hadn't magically morphed into something meaningful all on its own.

"You just haven't found your purpose yet," Jackie had told me one morning over the phone.

"My purpose?" My eyes practically rolled out of my head.

"Yes. That thing, or person, who's going to make you want to be a better man."

I snorted. "You don't think I'm a good man now?"

Her voice dropped to a whisper. "I think you have the potential to be so much more than you are."

I wasn't convinced of the potential part, but I did feel like I was stuck in a rut. For the last ten years, I'd been on autopilot, surviving from day to day. I woke up, went to work, headed to the bar, and then back home. That was it.

There had to be more to life than that. Right? I found I was craving someone to come home to at the end of a day— someone to talk to, to hold, and grow old with. It was sappy, but it was the truth.

I suppose that's why I relented to my sister's endless suggestions of online dating. So far, however, no one was turning my eye in the surrounding towns.

I deliberately left out the area I lived in on my search because besides knowing everyone here, there wasn't anything exciting about Bucksville. We had a population of just over a thousand people. There was one grocery store and one fast food joint but three gas stations. Why we needed so many, I had no idea.

About the biggest excitement we had in Bucksville was that we had a movie star who vacationed here from time to time. She lived up in a big-ass mansion on Miller Street. The town went nuts when she bothered to show her face to the locals, but thankfully, that wasn't often. My staff still liked to talk about the day she had come into the shop for coffee. I definitely didn't want someone as high-maintenance as her. I wanted a woman who'd look hot in both heels and sweats and who'd steal a slice of pizza out of my hands. It wouldn't hurt if she loved hockey, either. Could I say that in the ad? Probably make me look like a jackass.

I shook my head at the waiting cursor on my computer screen and blew out a breath of defeat. This was getting nowhere. I closed my laptop and focused on the waiting pile of bills on my desk. I shouldn't really call it a desk. It's a card table tucked into the former walk-in pantry I'd converted into an office. It wasn't pretty, but it did the trick.

As I cut checks, I fought off a yawn. It was late. The shop had long since closed. I wanted to go home, have a beer, maybe watch some porn, and go to bed. That was the sucky part of being a shop owner. Bills had to be tended to regardless of what I wanted.

I spent several aggravating minutes shoving paid invoices into the overstuffed filing cabinet in the corner. I cursed myself for not going digital. One of these days, I'd take the time and do it, but I didn't have the patience to learn a new way when the old one worked just fine.

Christ, I'm starting to sound like my dad.

When I reached the bottom of the waiting envelopes, I noticed it wasn't another bill but rather a letter. The envelope only said "Finn" on the outside.

Tearing it open, I adjusted my glasses to read the small handprint, which looked like it was scribbled down in haste.

I recognized the writing as Kenny's. Kenny was my only full-time barista. He was the real reason the shop did so well. That man knew how to make a mean cup of coffee. Kenny trained all the other part-timers how to use the machines, but none of them were particularly good at it. I knew I should give him a raise, but the funds weren't there.

Curious about why he'd write me a letter versus talking to me in the morning, I tore it open and skimmed over his words. I clutched my stomach as it rolled over. It was his letter of resignation. He'd taken a better paying job at a shop the next town over. It was closer to his daughter's school and offered him medical coverage.

"Shit."

I couldn't counter that offer.

The letter was his two-week notice. I had fourteen days to find a barista willing to work full-time for a measly minimum wage job with no benefits.

Opening my laptop again, I went to our community bulletin board website to post a help-wanted ad. I began it with the line MUST LOVE COFFEE.

Chapter 2

I was on my second espresso of the morning and about ready to bang my head straight through my laptop screen trying to find Kenny's replacement. This was a bad dream, or I was being Punk'd. That had to be the reason behind the string of horrific interviews the week after Kenny quit. Three weeks! It had been three weeks and I had yet to get someone to replace Kenny.

Ideally, I had wanted to hire someone right away so he'd have time to train them before he left. However, the ad ran for three days and there were no applications. Zero. Nada. It was only when I upped the pay by fifty cents an hour that a pathetic few applications came in. None had been an ideal candidate. They were all shit. But a warm body was better than no body. In theory.

At present, it was a toss-up between a high school senior who could only work a few months until he left for college, or the guy who put under his special skills: 'Knows how to use a hula hoop.'

I was on my tenth interview of the day. It felt like I was being punished. For what, though, I wasn't sure.

Rubbing the newest burn on my wrist, I looked down at the scorch marks that peppered my skin. I'd burned myself almost daily now trying to figure out the damn foam machine. That cursed machine was the only reason I was drinking espresso instead of my normal foam latte. My other employees attempted achieving the perfect foam, but the peaks always fell flat. Much like this job search.

Glancing down at the time on my phone, I grunted. My last interview on the horizon was late. A no-show, most likely, as two of them had been so far.

What was I going to do? I couldn't keep burning the candle at both ends. My other staff had already taken on as many hours as they could. If I didn't get a kick-ass barista soon, the business was going to suffer. Everything was riding on this last candidate: Sam Whitman. His résumé was, by far, the best of the bunch. He'd actually worked in a coffee house before, which was always promising. Not a lot of work history, though, so the guy must be young. Hopefully he was out of college. I didn't want to have to go through this search again any time soon.

"Finn?" Rebecca said, popping her head into my office. "She's here."

"Who's here?" I put down Sam's résumé and looked up at Rebecca's face riddled with acne. Poor kid. She would have a rough time in college in a few years.

"Your interview."

I stood up. "Wait. *She*?" I looked back at the paper on my desk. "Sam is a girl?"

Rebecca shrugged. "She has boobs."

I frowned at her bluntness.

"Okay, um—show her in then." I tried to tidy up my desk. Women tended to notice a mess more than the guys, and I couldn't afford to screw up this interview.

As I was dumping a slice of leftover pizza into the trash, I knew I was in trouble. A gorgeous brunette with dimples, olive-colored skin, and the lushest lips I'd ever seen stood before me. For a half a second, I thought God had answered my prayers and hand delivered the perfect woman for me. When she met my eyes and said, "Hello," I knew it was the

Devil's work instead. I knew her. We went to college together and I hated her.

I glared at her. "Samantha Matthews. I never thought I'd see you again."

She cocked her head to the side as though realizing I knew her. "It's Whitman now." She began to twirl her wedding ring, a thing women did when they wanted to remind a guy not to flirt with them. *She had no reason to worry. I wasn't going to flirt with her, let alone hire her. There was no way I was going to take on that pretentious bitch.*

Man, I loathed her in college. She was a busybody know-it-all. Her hand was always first to go up whenever the professor asked a question. She turned in her papers ahead of time, and got nothing but As, which threw off the bell curve. She was a thorn in my side, always looking down her nose at me. It didn't take a rocket scientist to know she didn't approve of how quickly I went through girls. Or maybe she was jealous I never asked her out?

The one question burning in the back of my mind—aside from when the hell did she get so hot—was why the class valedictorian was searching for a crap job like this. A small smile spread across my face. Oh, how the mighty had fallen.

"So, Samantha, what brings you back to the Bucksville area?" I heard myself ask, dying to know how her life had failed so epically.

"I'm sorry, how do we know each other?" Sam blinked up at me, wiping the smirk off my face. Was she serious? She didn't remember me?

"You're kidding, right?"

The look on her face let me know she wasn't playing. I'd made zero impact on her from college. That only made me angrier.

I rubbed at the back of my head to contain my frustration. As I did I noticed my gut overlapping my belt and sighed. Of course she didn't recognize me. I hardly did anymore. I removed my glasses. "Try to imagine me about ten pounds lighter and with hair." I had to admit, I'd changed since college, but so had she. If she'd looked even a fraction as hot then as she did now, she sure as hell would have remembered my name.

"I'm sorry...I still can't figure it out." Her voice was a lot huskier than I remembered it. Deep and sexy as hell.

I put my glasses back on and risked a glance down her body as she tried to place me. Time had been kinder to

Samantha than it had been to me. For one thing, she now had curves in all the right places which wasn't quite how I remembered her, but memory was a funny thing. Had she always been this good looking? Her hair had grown out from the pixie cut she used to wear. Now, it fell in lush black waves over her shoulders, stopping right at the nipples. Not that I was checking out her chest, mind you. Much. I ripped my eyes upward to focus on a safer spot, her deep chocolate eyes that were rimmed with laugh lines. I don't know why women tried to cover those up. They were one of my favorite parts on a woman.

"I'm sorry," Samantha finally said. "I give up. How do I know you?"

"It's Finn. Finn Allen?" I held out my hand for an awkward reintroduction handshake.

She took my hand and smiled in such a way that indicated she still didn't know who I was, but was trying to be polite.

"We went to college together?" I added. "You were in like five of my classes…"

Relief spread across her face.

"That explains it, then. Those years were sort of a blur. I don't remember much about college."

"Neither do I, but I remember you," I admitted, gesturing to the seat across from my still messy desk.

She took the proffered spot, and either didn't notice the arm of the chair was held together with duct tape, or didn't care.

"I'm afraid I was a bit self-absorbed back then," Samantha confessed. "I was friends with my books, not the people around me." She made a face that indicated she was frustrated with her past life. I could relate, to an extent. I'd done quite a few things, well…women I probably shouldn't have.

"You were the smartest girl on campus," I said.

She gave me a tight smile. "Well, that was a long time ago."

I nodded. "Yes, it was." I smiled again at her a moment before shifting into manager mode. "So, Samantha—"

"Sam, please."

"Okay then, Sam, your résumé is quite impressive."

Sam clasped her hands together and placed them on her lap. "Yes. As you can see I have management training and the skills needed for the job."

"Yes. Some might say you're too qualified," I said, still trying to figure out why she wanted this job.

Sam's face shifted into business mode. "I understand that some employers see my strong work ethic as a sign I won't remain in their employ for long. But let me assure you, Mr. Allen, I have no plans to leave the area anytime soon in search of my fame and fortune in the coffee industry elsewhere."

I couldn't help but laugh. She had spunk. I had to give her that. "There's the Sam I remember. A straight shooter. You haven't changed a bit."

"Oh, I wouldn't say that," she said with a light tone and yet felt incredibly sad at the same time.

"Always so headstrong," I continued. "You knew what you wanted in life and went after it." She had the conviction I lacked. That's probably why I'd hated her.

She nodded. "Agreed. And I want this job, Mr. Allen." Her desire for the job I could see. It was the *why* she wanted it that was the mystery I wanted to figure out.

"If I have to call you Sam, you need to call me Finn. Mr. Allen makes me feel, well, old."

Her face softened. "Of course, Finn. I can be flexible on my hours, if need be," Sam said, pulling out a slip of paper with writing on it. "I do, however, need some nights off."

Laughter erupted from my lips at her boldness. "Assuming I hire you, that is?"

She sat up straighter. "I don't need to assume. You will hire me."

My eyebrows shot up, and I leaned across the desk. "And why is that?" I knew my tone was flirty, but damn it all if her boldness wasn't exciting.

"Because, Finn, I'll be the hardest working employee you have. I'll show up on time every day. I know how to work a register, treat customers right, and can brew a cup of coffee like no one's business."

I nodded to each of her points.

"And besides," she went on, "I'm way too qualified for it, so you better nab me now before I go across town to try my luck there."

Damn. Why did I find her fierce determination such a turn off back then? The drive in her eyes was hot as hell.

"I believe you were telling me about your work conflicts," I said in my best professional voice.

There was no mistaking the small smirk that crept onto her face before her business face returned.

"I can't stay past five p.m. on Monday, Wednesday, Friday, and Sundays. There can be no exception to those days."

"Is that so?" I said, not mentioning I was looking for morning coverage anyway. "Mind if I ask why?"

"Actually, I do mind. My personal life is my own if that's all the same to you."

I guess getting to know her was off the table.

She blinked at me, waiting for my reply while I pondered her hire. On the one hand, she sure was fun to look at. On the other hand, could I really deal with what might be the world's largest attitude? Rack or not, that could get tiresome.

Sam must have sensed my annoyance because she leaned forward in the chair.

"I know my schedule might prove difficult to accommodate, but I am a hard worker. I go above and beyond what is expected."

"I'm sure you do." I scratched the back of my neck. On paper, she was the best of all of the applicants, but I wasn't sure our personalities would jive.

Still, I needed an employee. I needed one three weeks ago.

"I guess I only have one question," I said, giving up.

Sam took in a breath of anticipation.

"Do you love coffee?" I smiled at my own bad joke.

"God, no." She made a face. "Can't stand the stuff."

"Um, you do know the name of my store is called Must Love Coffee, right?"

Without blinking, she answered. "A person doesn't need to enjoy coffee in order to make the perfect hot beverage."

I narrowed my eyes at her.

"Let me guess, you're a tea lover?" They were the worst sort of person. I felt myself shiver.

"I do drink tea, yes." Her voice was strong.

"All right, tea traitor, how do you make a Dirty Chai Tea, then?" I was testing her knowledge, for sure, but I also wanted to see how she was under pressure.

She sat up a bit taller, as though reciting an answer in a classroom. "You start with the tea. Add the customer's preferred milk product, steamed is best, though, a shot of espresso, then dust the top with cinnamon and sugar."

"How about an Appogato?"

"It's also called a Glacé. You put two scoops of very cold ice cream into a coffee cup—it can't be that soft-serve crap—and a double shot of espresso. Top that with shaved dark chocolate and/or chopped hazelnuts. Depending on how the management wishes it to be prepared."

The look in her eye told me she could do this all day. That shouldn't have surprised me. She was a bookworm, after all, and she would have studied for this test.

I contemplated my answer for a moment. In a fraction of a second, I saw Sam's mask slip. On the outside, she appeared to be calm, cool, and collected. It was only when she looked down at the ground that I sensed a desperation buried there: a sincere need for a job, any job. It would be a pity to send someone so beautif—talented somewhere else.

Letting out a breath, I said, "When can you start?"

 Chapter 3

My ass was dragging. I wasn't used to these early mornings. I didn't even take the time for coffee. I literally rolled out of bed, threw on some cloths, and headed downstairs to work. Sam was waiting outside the shop when I trudged my way down the steps at 4:35, tapping her foot.

"You're late," Sam said, pulling her light jacket tight around her. It wasn't October yet, but the nights had definitely taken on a chill that lingered until mid-morning.

I looked at my watch. "By five minutes."

Sam frowned. "If you expect your employees to be here at four thirty you should be here fifteen minutes prior. The lights should be on, the temperature set. Machines turned on. Pastries need to be put out," she rattled off tasks with a tone belonging to someone clearly trained in management.

"Yeah, well, I'm the owner, and I get here when I get here, and you'll deal with it or you won't get a paycheck," I snapped.

Sam's demeanor changed on a dime to one of a woman in danger of losing her job. I felt like a dick.

"I'm sorry," I said, unlocking the door. "I'm used to dealing with rebellious teens who never show on time and I'm extremely grumpy before coffee."

Sam nodded but didn't say anything further.

My eyes squinted when the lights flicked on. Yawning as I walked, I began to switch on the machines for the day.

"Sandy will be working with you for most of the day, but she doesn't get in until ten." I pulled out the morning food items from the cooler. "She drives her friends at the nursing home to the grocery store on Sunday mornings, which is why you'll open Sunday. You needed those nights off anyway, yes?"

Sam nodded as she pulled out a pair of disposable gloves and helped me place the muffins and scones in the display case without any instruction. "The nights, yes, but I can open on Sundays, no problem."

After the food was sorted, she took off her jacket but offered up no additional information. I was impressed that she was wearing the black button-up and tan pants I'd indicated were the uniform. Most of my employees took their sweet time complying.

Her hair was pulled back into a ponytail, which highlighted her round, apple-dusted cheeks. Tiny diamond studs kissed each ear, and her lips had only the faintest hint of lip gloss. I'd never been a fan of lip gloss, but right in that moment, I couldn't help but wonder what it might feel like to kiss that shine right off her lips—

"Hello? Earth to Mr. Allen?"

Blinking, I realized she'd asked a question while I'd been busy staring at her lips.

"I'm sorry, what did you say? Pre-coffee brain. And remember, call me Finn."

"I asked if there was an apron I could use."

"Right. Sorry. Um, yeah, let me just…" I walked over to Sam, who was standing in the narrow galley of the prep area. There wasn't a lot of room to move. So, I did my best to reach around her to grab the apron, but I managed to graze the side of her left breast in the process. Or had she moved closer to me on purpose? I couldn't be sure, but I played it cool, as though nothing had happened.

She was a married woman, after all. I had to behave. Besides, I didn't even like her. She was annoying. Or at least, she used to be. I had no idea what she was like now, besides determined.

"Dirty ones go in the bin at the end of the counter by the biscotti display."

Sam nodded and placed on her apron with ease. I was a bit less elegant when putting mine on, as I hadn't quite mastered the tying-behind-my-back-thing.

"I need coffee before I show you the rest."

Sam rolled her eyes. "What do you want?"

"You're going to make me my coffee?" I asked.

"If it means I can be trained before customers actually come in, then yes."

I waved a dismissive hand. "Don't worry about customers. We don't get our rush until nine. We'll get a few locals, but most of our traffic is before and after church."

She picked up a mug. "I'm still waiting for your order."

Sam was a no-nonsense sort of lady. I wasn't at all surprised.

"A latte. Whole milk, please, chocolate dusting on the foam."

Sam gave me a tight smile and set to work. A few moments later, she set down a nice steaming mug at the table where I'd collapsed to catch a few more Zs. Clearly, I was still not used to waking up this early. Kenny had always opened. I was a night owl, so I always closed. Now, I was doing both shifts most nights and I was exhausted. Fighting back another yawn, I looked down at the frothy tip in the cup and smiled.

"I love you, coffee," I whispered to the mug.

"No, you don't."

Frowning, I glanced up at Sam. "I beg your pardon?"

"You don't love coffee."

"Um, yes, I do."

She shook her head, tossing the black waves in her ponytail to and fro. "No, you don't. You're addicted to it, sure, but you don't love it."

I scoffed. "Same difference."

"Wrong. You can't love something you're addicted to. You can only be controlled by it."

My eyebrows pulled together, annoyed.

Sam looked at me a moment, as though debating saying something. She blew her hair out of her eyes then pulled out the chair next to me and sat down. "Love is more than filling some random need."

I gave her at blank stare, so she went on.

"You can replace coffee with any caffeinated beverage and your addiction is still unaffected."

I nodded, despite wanting to object, but her logic was sound. "I'm with you so far…" I said, trying to keep the conversation going.

Her eyes wandered off, lost in some memory that wasn't here.

"You can't say the same thing about love. You can't replace a person you love with some other random person and remain unaffected." By the end of her sentence, her eyes had welled with tears. "Therefore, you can *like* coffee, Finn, but you can't *love* it. Not really."

With that, she got up and walked away, leaving me to stare down at my deflating foam.

"Don't listen to her, coffee. You and I will always be together," I said before taking a tentative first sip. "Mmm." It was good. Better than Kenny's.

I glanced up at Sam, who was wiping off the machines she'd used before I looked back at my cup. I gave a nod backward toward Sam and muttered to the cup, "I bet she'd be a lot better in the sack than you, though."

"I heard that," Sam said, throwing the rag over her shoulder.

Heat filled my cheeks. "Um…that was a joke. Honest."

As she walked over, her arms crossed, I saw visions of sexual harassment lawsuits approaching. "Are you insinuating, then, that the coffee would be better in the sack than I am?"

"What? No, I just meant…"

Wetting her lips, intentionally or not, she lowered her body down, allowing the briefest glimpse of her cleavage. My eyes followed without my consent. Yup, I was definitely going to get sued.

"It isn't a joke then. Either I'd be better in the sack than your coffee or I wouldn't. Which is it?"

I raised my hands in surrender. "Whatever answer is going to get me in the least trouble."

She stood up and snickered. "Have fun with your coffee." Throwing me a backward glance, she went back to cleaning the machines.

Confused, I watched her. I couldn't figure her out. She was both hot and cold, which meant this could either end really well, or really, really bad.

 Chapter 4

For the next several minutes, I showed Sam the ropes. Not that she needed it. She was an incredibly fast learner, oftentimes showing me more efficient ways to do things. It was obvious she was smart, which confused me. Why was she working a minimum-wage job when she had a college degree and management skills?

I turned on our open sign and then leaned against the edge of one of the tables, still not fully awake.

"You shouldn't sit on the tables," Sam tsked. "People eat there." She shoved me off with a push from her shoulder and proceeded to wipe the table down.

I laughed at the gesture. "You know, I can't figure you out."

Sam straightened her shoulders and pulled herself up to her five-foot-four stature. Even slouching, I towered over her, which I sort of liked. I could cocoon her in my arms with ease if I wanted.

Whoa. Dude. That's not what you want, so get a grip. I shook my head to get that mental picture out of my mind. Mercifully, Sam didn't seem to notice my daydreaming.

"What's to figure out?" she asked. "You needed a barista, I applied. You hired me. Case closed."

"Yeah, but there's something else going on with you," I said. "Normally, I can read a person at first glance, but you…you have me scratching my head."

Sam gave me a tight smile. "I didn't realize knowing a person's backstory was necessary to do a job properly. Is that grounds for firing here?"

"Fire you? Are you kidding? In the last few minutes you've learned more than half of my staff did in a month."

She gave me a short, firm nod, as though satisfied with that answer. "Good. If there's ever an issue with my performance, please don't hesitate to let me know. I'll do better."

There was something about her face that struck me just then. She was scared. No, scared is the wrong word. She seemed downright terrified she was going to be let go.

I walked over and took her elbow lightly.

She jumped and looked up into my eyes.

"I'm not going to fire you. So long as you show up and do the work, you have a job here. Understood?"

Her bottom lip trembled, but she nodded quickly.

The door jingled open at that moment as a customer came in. Sam pulled away from me as I walked to the register but not before noticing Sam wiping away a tear.

She recovered in a matter of seconds and was smiling politely at Mr. Weston, a local real estate attorney who always got a large black coffee, two sugars, and a bran muffin.

Sam took the lead on the sale and rang Mr. Weston up with no issues. She had this down.

"Mind if I make a quick call?" she asked after Mr. Weston left.

"Sure."

I was about to offer her some tea or a muffin before she did, but she grabbed her coat and was outside and on her cell before I had the chance.

By the way she was smiling, she was probably talking to her husband. I couldn't help the small pang of jealousy that struck me. All the viable women in this town were taken or trouble. Not that I had any notions of starting anything with Sam, even if she had been single.

Still, just because Sam was unavailable in a romantic way, I couldn't shake the feeling that she needed help. She was sending out a strong vibe that she was in distress, and I wanted to know why and, more importantly, how I could make it better.

People could say what they wanted about me and my past, but if someone needed help, I was always the first one in line. Except for those dark weeks after my folks died. Back then I was pretty much useless to everyone, but after that, I wanted to fix whatever was broken. There was something broken about Sam, and I wanted to make it better.

Sam came back from her call and made no indication of who she'd spoken to, not that she owed me that information. She busied herself by loading the dishwasher and drying mugs while I re-loaded up the pastry display.

"So, Sam, how long have you been married?" I asked as casually as I could while brushing crumbs off the counter.

She stiffened at the question.

"Twenty-three years." Her words came out soft, as though she couldn't believe how much time had passed.

"Wow. Congratulations. That's a long time. I don't think I've ever been committed to anything for that long." I scratched my head. "Maybe a toaster once…"

She smiled at my lame joke. "We married fresh out of college. It was a long time ago, for sure."

"Funny. I don't remember you dating anyone in college."

Sam looked up from the mug she was drying. "You paid attention to who I was dating back then?"

"No, I guess not. I was a bit…preoccupied myself in college, but I'd remember if you were dating someone."

She frowned and tossed the towel she was using over her shoulder and folded her arms across her chest.

"And why would you remember that?" She narrowed her eyes. "I mean, it's not like we were close. Why would you remember anything about me?"

I made a pained face. "Because I…loathed you."

Her eyebrows shot up. "You *loathed* me?" There was a definite layer of hurt in her question.

I shrugged my shoulders. "You were just so smart. It pissed me off, I guess. I was a punk kid. What did I know?"

Her eyes softened for a moment, then she lowered her head.

"Well, that was a long time ago. Things change."

I wanted to ask more about that statement, but Sandy came in then. Our conversation came to a close in favor of the obligatory introductions.

After the post-church rush, I opted to let Sandy take the lead with Sam's training while I went back into the office to call vendors. Most of them were closed on a Sunday, but I was so distracted I called a few I knew would be closed by mistake. I would have much rather stayed and worked side by side with Sam, but as it was, we were down to our last order of muffins. If I didn't reach the bakery soon there wouldn't be enough to last the week. Happy coffee drinkers are fed coffee drinkers. If the bakery ever picked up their phone, I'd be able to have an order delivered by Tuesday. It was time to put on the owner hat and get down to work.

With each call I made, however, my attention wandered out to the front. I kept craning my neck in a painful position to catch a glimpse of Sam. I told myself it was only to make sure she was doing well and nothing more. So then why did my heart do this weird flip-flop thing whenever I caught her eye?

Sam's shift ended at 1:30 p.m., and I had wanted to touch base with her before she left, but I was stuck on a damn call.

Rebecca was in and working the register when I came out, so I took that opportunity to check on Sam's progress with Sandy.

"How'd she do?" I asked, filling up an empty cup with some freshly brewed decaf. My nerves were shot, so it was time to switch to something uncaffeinated.

Sandy frowned and placed her long, thin hands on her hips. Her blue-gray veins bulged out from her nearly translucent skin. A telltale sign of her advancing age. She may be close to retirement, but she had a feisty nature I was about to get a taste of. "Is there something you want to tell me?"

"I beg your pardon?"

"Are you unsatisfied with my work?" Sandy asked.

"Your work? No. What are you talking about?"

Sandy slapped her towel onto the counter.

"I know I'm no spring chicken anymore, so you don't need to beat around the bush." She tapped her foot impatiently.

"Huh?"

"What's the deal with the new chick?" she said as though that explained everything.

I made a face. "Is she not working out? Did she do something? I can work with her, train her more—"

"Oh, she's working out fine. So fine, in fact, that pretty soon you aren't gonna need me."

That was not the answer I was expecting.

"How do you figure?"

"That girl is sharp as a tack, Finn. She only needs to be told how to do something once. Once." Sandy took back her towel and began to ring it ever so gently. "She does the work of two, easy."

"I see," I said, not understanding at all.

She frowned. "Is that your plan, then? Get me to train her then show me the door?"

Ah. There it is. I rubbed my hands over my face. "No, Sandy. That's not my goal. Kenny quit. We needed more help. End of story."

"You're not gonna give her more shifts? *My* shifts?" Sandy's painted on eyebrows shot up.

"No, Sandy. Your job is safe. Sam is a part-time worker. I don't think barista-world-domination is on her list of things to do."

Sandy looked over her shoulder at an approaching customer. "Well, good. I got bills to pay, you know?"

"Yes, I know," I reassured her. "We all do."

That seemed to settle her nerves as she went back to work. I took that opportunity to slip outside with my cup for a few minutes. I was beat. I needed a nap before I worked later tonight, but for now, I'd settle for just being outdoors.

There was a chill, to be sure, but nothing I couldn't handle without my coat. Fall was my favorite time of year. Not too hot, not too cold, and the damn mosquitoes were dead. It was perfect.

As I sipped my java I leaned back in the chair and watched the people passing by, waving to the locals I knew. Life was simple here. I liked that, even though as a teenager it was the one thing I hated about the tiny town. Funny how things change as you get older…how what you want from life changes.

After my coffee, I straightened up the outside tables, clearing off a few stray cups that had been left behind. I was about to head back in when I saw Sam down the block out of the corner of my eye. She was a few doors down, looking into a shop window and chatting on her cell phone. Her face had a look of distress. As she talked, her eyes kept wandering over to the window longingly. Maybe she was fighting with her husband about wanting to make a purchase or something? I couldn't make out what shop she was looking at from here, which irritated me.

After a moment, she put her phone away. She took one last look at the window, then walked around the corner.

I'm not proud to admit this, but I took that opportunity to spy on her. I dumped the empty cups into the trash bin and walked down the sidewalk, trying to find where she had been.

There were a few non-descript doors that led to office spaces above the store fronts. It couldn't be those because her gaze never went upward. That left the drug store and the dance studio. It had to be one of these places. But which one?

The drugstore didn't have much in their window display as to convey a sense of longing. That only left Ms. CeCe's Salsa Studio. *Huh. Could that be it?* Was she arguing with her husband to take classes with her? Had he turned her down? Had she wanted to go dancing? I tried to imagine her on the dance floor. High heels, her hips fitting snugly in a black dress…

Without thinking about logistics, I walked into the dance studio and signed up for couples Salsa lessons. I didn't give a rat's ass about dancing, but if it would make Sam happy, then it seemed like the right thing to do. The first class was next Sunday.

A week. That's how long I'd have to convince Sam she should take a dance class with me.

Yup. I'd officially lost my mind.

Chapter 5

When I came back in from outside I looked at the clock and noticed Tina still hadn't showed. She was consistently late, even if she was closing. Huffing, I pulled on an apron to cover for her. This was getting really old.

"That's it. I'm calling her," I said.

Sandy looked at me in shock. I'd never said anything when Tina was late in the past.

I went into my office to use the phone there in case I had to raise my voice. I was just about to dial her number when a light knock sounded on my door.

"Be right out, Sandy."

"It's not Sandy. It's me," a small voice said.

"Sam?" I said, turning around. "You're back. What's up?"

"Sorry. I forgot to clock out earlier. My mind was on other things. Sorry."

"Oh. Right. Um. That's okay. I don't actually have a formal time-clock anyway. I sort of go on the honor system here."

"That can lead to chronically tardy employees."

I nodded. "Yeah. It sure can. But really, it's fine. You look exhausted. Go home. Get some rest."

"I'm not going home. I have other obligations I must tend to. Sorry for the confusion."

Confusion was right. She looked out of sorts.

"Well. See you tomorrow," I said.

"Four thirty. Sharp," came her reply.

She turned then and walked out of my office. I followed after, trying to be natural by clearing a few tables. I watched her as she left the shop and began her descent down Main Street. Her light jacket, pulled tight around her waist, her head bowed low against the wind. I worked my way to the window tables, grabbing a rag to wipe down an already clean table just so I could see what sort of car she drove, but she disappeared at the next block before I could find out.

"Sorry, sorry. I know I'm late!" Tina said, walking through the door looking like she'd just crawled out of bed.

"You're thirty-five minutes late," I said, tossing the rag over my shoulder.

She walked over to me and bit her bottom lip, her eyes, doe-like as she blinked at me. Those damn perky breasts of hers heaved high to try to confuse my mind.

"I slept through my alarm."

Ripping my eyes off her chest, I glared at her. "It's the middle of afternoon, Tina. This can't keep happening."

Her face crumpled into a frown. "Oh, don't be such a hard-ass." She leaned in close to me. "Or you won't get to have access to this hard ass anymore." She winked and sauntered over to the counter, being sure to wiggle her hips in the way she knew I liked.

I'd crossed the line when I screwed her last month, but her body was rock-solid…and that ass—damn. She was the only employee I allowed to wear jeans simply because I loved the way she filled them out, but now? I found myself disgusted, mostly at myself.

"Tina? Can I see you in the office for a moment?"

She snapped her gum and looked at me, her pierced eyebrow arched upward in a suggestive way. She probably thought I was finally going to ask her to screw in my office while the shop was open. It was a thought that had crossed my mind on more than one occasion. I'll admit I'd fantasized about taking her there a million times, but currently it was the furthest thing from my mind.

"Now," I barked.

That got her attention. "Yes, sir." She smirked and followed after me into the office.

"Have a seat," I said, gesturing to the chair. I turned to close the door and, a moment later, her hands wormed up through my shirt.

"Jesus, Tina," I cursed, shoving her off. "Knock it off."

Her eyes widened in disbelief. "What's your problem?"

I pinched the bridge of my nose and tried to focus. I walked over to my desk and sat down, putting as much room between the two of us as possible. "Please, sit."

"Yes, sir," she purred, clearly thinking I was playing.

"No. Look, Tina, don't get the wrong idea here. I need to talk to you about a few things."

Batting her eyelashes, she sat seductively on the chair, pulling her arms in close to her side to make her cleavage show. "What's up, Finny?"

I flinched. I used to like it when she called me that, but now it felt…gross. "It's Finn or Mr. Allen, for starters."

She sucked in a bubble she was blowing with a loud smack.

"Look, it's time you started being more professional." I gestured to her chest area. "I need you to button up at least two more buttons, start wearing the khakis, like the rest of us, and above all else, I need you to show up on time."

The look Tina gave me was nothing short of shocked amusement.

"Are you for real?"

"I am."

"But you love me in jeans." She smirked, leaning her chest area dangerously close across the desk. "And out of them."

I pushed back in the chair to escape her proximity.

"Not anymore. I'm turning a new leaf. It's time I acted my age. As should you. You're twenty-seven years old, Tina. It's time to start behaving like a lady instead of a two-bit whore."

The words slipped out of my mouth before I even considered how they might sound.

"Screw you, asshole," she said, tossing her apron and key onto my desk. "I quit."

"Tina!" My voice lost steam as she left the room. Did I really want to deal with her drama? On the other hand, I'd only just replaced Kenny and that had taken forever. I didn't want to have to endure that nightmare again.

Unless…unless I took Tina's shifts. I was already doing double duty and Tina's shifts would be way easier for me to swing than Kenny's had been. So what if several of Tina's shifts happened to be with Sam? That was just a coincidence.

"Well, that meeting didn't go as planned," I muttered to my empty office. I waited for the jingle on the door to chime signaling Tina's departure before going out to the front.

"Tina go home sick?" Sandy asked a moment after passing an Americano to a customer, knowing instantly there was gossip to be had.

"She quit."

"Quit? Why?"

I shrugged my shoulders. "I got tired of her strutting around like an overgrown teeny-bopper. I told her to start dressing appropriately and show up on time. She opted to be a child and quit."

Sandy looked over her glasses at me. "Who are you?"

"I know, I know." I raised my hands in surrender. "I guess I've grown up."

"Mmhmm, or you've set your sights on an older woman."

I blushed but began loading cups into the dishwasher to avoid her poking her nose into where it didn't belong.

Sandy leaned down low, following me, and whispered, "It's me, isn't it?"

My eyes bugged out of my head, causing Sandy to break out into her famous snort-laugh. A few customers glanced up from their phones to give either a look of amusement or annoyance.

After her laughter died down, Sandy's face grew serious.

"Now, Finn, you know I love you like one of my own boys, but I'm telling you, don't get yourself caught up in something with Sam."

"What? No, I'm—"

She held up her hand. "Don't try to deny it. I've seen you craning your neck out of your office all damn day trying to take a peek at her."

"I was only checking on how she was doing, that's all."

Sandy wasn't buying it. "You never watched over any of the rest of us like that. Well, that's not true, you hovered around Tina, but I suspect you were thinking with your balls and not your heart on that one."

I was shocked by her brazenness and her keen eye. Apparently, I wasn't as subtle as I thought I was. I'd have to watch that in the future—especially where Sam was concerned.

"You're a sweet guy, Finn, somewhere underneath your old horn-dog ways." She smiled at me. "And Sam is a nice woman, as far as I can tell," Sandy continued, her smile fading. "But she's also a married one. I've seen the rock on her hand. Tread carefully, Finn. Very, very carefully."

"I know that, Sandy. And I'm not interested in her. Honest."

Sandy crossed her arms, clearly not believing me.

"I'm not. Seriously. If I were interested in her, would I have set up an online dating profile?"

Sandy didn't have to know I hadn't actually made my profile live yet. I had meant to, but things got too busy after Kenny quit...*And then Sam walked into your life and made everything confusing.*

"Oh, God. My niece tried to set me up on one of those. The men on there were pigs." She made a face and leaned in. "Grown men in their sixties sending me pictures of their you-know-whats." She shook her head. "Don't do that sort of thing, you hear?"

I laughed, picturing Sandy opening up an unsolicited dick pic. "Yeah, I won't do that. That's gross."

She glanced around to make sure no one was listening and whispered low to me, "You know, no one likes the look of those things. Why else do you think God made them to go *inside* a woman where they can't be seen? Hmm? Vile looking things."

I began to bust a gut while she left to bus some tables. You could always count on Sandy to give it to you straight, and she wanted it known that Sam was off the table. I knew that. Of course I knew.

Anything I had with Sam would be platonic. Point blank. However, there wasn't any harm in giving her those dance lessons, was there? As a friend. I only wanted to make her smile, that's all. What could possibly be the harm in that?

Chapter 6

The next morning, I was early for my shift, by a full ten minutes. No one was more shocked at that than me. I was inside, flicking on the machines when Sam came through the door. She wore that same thin jacket as yesterday even though the temperature was twenty degrees colder today. That's how it was in the fall, though. Some days you froze your ass off, others you sat in front of the AC. Even so, she looked rather cold.

"Morning," she said, taking off her coat, revealing her uniform underneath. Gooseflesh erupted on her skin from the remaining chill outside.

After she hung up her jacket, I tried to offer her some coffee.

"You sure you don't want some?" I asked, opening the large plastic tub that held the coffee beans.

"Ugh, no. Thank you." Her face crumpled up as she turned away from the smell. Something red on the edge of her pants drew my attention.

"Oh, looks like you got something on your pant leg, right there, by your ankle."

Sam turned to see what I was talking about.

"Wait, is that blood?" It very much looked like it. A big, fat drop of it. I looked up at her, scanning for any visible cuts where she may have bled from, but saw nothing but her bloodshot eyes staring back at me.

"I must have cut my leg shaving this morning." Her answer was fast, clipped. "Hey, wasn't I supposed to be opening with a girl named Tina today? Sandy told me not to bother coming in so early since she was never on time."

She was changing the subject, but I decided to let it drop.

"Um, yeah, you were, but she sort of quit yesterday."

Sam nodded once as if that was all the explanation needed.

"If you need me to take on other shifts, I can, but I have certain times I need off." She bent over to bring up the coffee filters from under the counter but had to stop midway down.

She clutched the counter with one hand to steady a sudden loss of balance.

"Whoa, you okay?" I rushed over to her, spilling some of the beans from the container I'd been holding. She was pale, almost as though she were going to faint. "Easy," I said, taking her under the elbow and guiding her to a seat.

"I'm okay," she protested. "I moved too fast, that's all."

I pressed my hand to her forehead to check for a fever, but her temperature seemed normal. If anything, she seemed cool to the touch.

"Have you eaten anything yet?" I asked, knowing that sometimes I got light-headed myself when I was busy.

"I have." She blinked several times as though willing the blood to rush back into her body.

"What did you have? Maybe it didn't sit right?"

"Um, I had some bread and a few bites of mashed potatoes..." Her voice sounded far off.

"For breakfast?"

She looked up at me. "Oh, no. That was at lunch yesterday." A weak smile spread across her lips. "I guess time got away from me."

So that explained why she looked so weak. She was hungry.

"That does it. I'm going to get you a muffin and some tea." I held up a hand to her protesting. "And you're not going to move from this spot until you've finished it. Understood?"

She gave me a firm look but finally nodded. "Thank you, Mr. Allen."

"It's Finn," I reminded her. "And you're welcome. Besides, you'll actually be doing me a favor."

"Oh?"

"Yeah," I said, putting a fat blueberry muffin topped with large chunks of granulated sugar on a plate. "The bakery dropped off a few samples of a new recipe for blueberry muffins last night. You can be one of the first to try one out." I placed the plate in front of her, then busied myself with getting her tea ready.

"Oh, I don't want to eat a limited supply of muffins. Just give me whatever is the stalest," she said.

"Well, they wouldn't be so limited if I hadn't had one or three last night." I coughed a bit while she chuckled.

Watching her from behind the counter, I saw her rip off a chunk of the muffin crown and pop it into her mouth.

"Mmm. This is very good," she said between chews.

"Yeah, I thought so, too." I padded the roundness of my belly and frowned a bit before sucking it in.

By the time her tea had steeped the muffin was all but gone.

"I guess I was hungrier than I thought," she admitted when I set down the tea in front of her.

"Or the muffins are just that good," I countered. "Would you like another? I know I would."

Without waiting for an answer I went back and grabbed the last two muffins. The customers could try them next week. Sam needed these calories more than they did.

"So," I said after a few minutes of silent chewing. "Were you serious about picking up some of Tina's shifts? I had a hard enough time hiring you. I figured I'd take her shifts for a while, but if you could use the money..." I was fishing. I knew that but hoped she didn't.

"More money is always good, isn't it?" she said, giving away nothing.

"Well, great. Maybe we can talk over schedules today, see what works for you? We could hash it out over lunch today?" I knew that suggestion was a bit ballsy on my part, but I sensed there was something on her mind and, for whatever reason, I really wanted to know what it was.

The light smile she was wearing left her face. Her eyes turned down, her hands slipping down to her lap. "I have plans for lunch. Sorry."

"Oh. Right. Well, we can try to find some time today to talk then, when it's quiet."

Sam began digging around in her purse. A moment later she pulled out a sheet of paper and slid it across to me. "These are the times I'm busy. If one of her shifts falls on a day I'm free, pencil me in."

I took the proffered paper without looking at it.

"I'll need that back, so don't lose it. The memory isn't what it used to be," she said, smiling. After a second, she stood up and grabbed our dishes. "Right, now it's time to get that coffee going."

I glanced at the clock and saw we'd wasted away a good chunk of our morning prep time. Shoving the paper into my back pocket, I went back to grind the coffee and dispose of the beans I'd spilled.

While I worked, I lamented my idiocy. I shouldn't have offered to have lunch with her. I felt horrible I'd overstepped, but I couldn't seem to stop myself when I was around her.

There was an unshakable sense that I needed to help her…protect her somehow.

I was still mulling these feelings over as the last drips of the French Roast landed into the carafe. Just in time, too. The jingle of the front door alerted us to the first customer of the day: Mr. Davenport. He came in every other day, promptly at five thirty to order a decaf—of all things—and a pastry. To go.

"Morning, Mr. Davenport. I've got you all set to go."

A nod was all I ever got from him, but today he stopped short and looked at Sam.

"Mrs. Whitman," he said. "I didn't know you worked here."

Her head lowered for a second, almost in shame. "I do. I just started. Time to start saving up for the holidays," she said with a smile that didn't seem real.

"Yes. Indeed. Well, I'll see you tonight still, yes?"

She nodded. "I'll be there."

He paid for his breakfast and lifted the pastry bag up in sort of a toast-like gesture to me, then left.

"What was that about?" I asked, knowing it was none of my damn business.

Sam gave me a look that told me as much, but after a quick huff she replied, "Nothing. I work for him."

"You work for Mr. Davenport?"

She snapped her head up. "Yeah? So?"

"Isn't he, like, a doctor or something?"

She licked her lips. "He's a dental surgeon. No, I'm not a dental hygienist or anything. I clean his office a few nights a week. You have a problem with that?"

"No. I, no... Not at all. I'm just surprised. Mr. Davenport is such a grouch. I didn't think anyone would willingly work for him, is all."

Her expression softened. "Oh, well, yes, he's a bit of a grump, but his checks don't bounce."

I wasn't sure why, but I reached out then and took her arm gently. "Mine won't either. I hope you know that."

She let her arm hover in my hand for a moment before she pulled away. "I do. Thank you."

The rest of the morning was too busy to talk about much more than utilitarian conversation. It was beyond frustrating. There was something going on with Sam, but I couldn't put my finger on it.

When there was a moment of quiet, I retreated to my office to order more muffins and go over the schedule.

The morning had been quite busy, but the two of us managed okay. If Tina had been working, there would have been a line for sure. Tina wasn't all that useful come to think of it. She was more eye-candy than anything. A distraction from what was important.

Digging into my back pocket, I pulled out the piece of paper Sam had given me and laid it out flat. On it was a grid of sorts. Monday through Sunday ran down the left-hand side. Time blocks ran along the top. Some things were in ink, others in pencil, but from what I could discern, there was very little time that was actually free. Not even for sleep. Squinting, I noticed that, according to this slip, she had worked at Mr. Davenport's the night before from 8:00 to 11:00 p.m. She had to be here at 4:30 a.m. That was hardly enough time to sleep. No wonder she was so tired.

Almost every block was full. There were a total of three jobs listed, too. All added up, her hours came to sixty-four hours a week, and she was willing to take on more shifts?

"Why does the smartest girl I knew in college need to work three jobs?" I asked in a light whisper. What the hell did that husband of hers do for a living that she needed to work so much?

If I'd been curious about her life story before, I was downright determined to find out the answers now.

Chapter 7

It had been a long few weeks and an even longer day. I'd worked not only Tina's shifts since she was let go but my own. Twelve hours on my feet night after night and I was ready to crash. Sam was doing great, though she seemed as tired as I was. I was getting used to having her around, and her smile when she greeted me in the morning was making these double shifts bearable.

I'd made it up the stairs and gotten the key in my apartment door when my cell went off. I sighed when I saw the number.

"What's up, Joe?" I asked, turning the key and letting myself in.

"Buddy," exclaimed the raspy voice. I could tell from the octave of his voice where Joe was calling from: the bar. "You haven't been down to the pub all week. What gives? You finally get yourself a piece of ass?" Judging by the slight slur of his words, I knew he'd been there for at least an hour.

"No, man. Crazy busy lately. Kenny quit and I've had to cover his shifts while I trained the new girl."

"New girl, eh? She hot?"

"Joe—"

His laugh came booming through my cell. "That wasn't a 'no!' Get your butt down here and tell me all about her. The guys are killing me at darts, and I need your arm."

I rubbed my face with my hand. "I don't know, Joe. It's been a long day. I've been up since four."

"All the more reason to come for a drink! Don't make me come to your place and drag you down here myself."

I had no doubt he'd do that. Joe could be quite demanding when he got wasted, and I certainly didn't want him on the roads in his condition.

"Fine. I'll come down for one round of darts, but then I'm out of there." It might be good to have a drink before bed, help quiet the noise in my head.

Twenty minutes later, while nursing a beer, I took aim at the dart board. As I was about to release it, a low whistle escaped from Joe.

"Looks like you sure as hell made that fox mad, Finn."

I followed Joe's eye to the bar where a very angry and drunk Tina glared at me. She started walking straight toward me, and I lowered the dart.

"Shit."

Joe cackled behind me as the rest of the guys joined in his laughter.

"Uh-oh, someone's in trouble," shouted Nick, Jackie's husband, a regular at the pub. The asshole loved to pick on me. A few more whistles came from behind as I walked over to Tina, hoping to get out of earshot from the peanut gallery.

"Well, look who it is? The guy who needs a 'lady' in his life."

I grimaced hearing my own words twisted around and thrown back at me. She took another step closer and brushed her body up against me. Those damn perfect breasts pressed hard on my chest.

She licked her big, pouty lips and whispered into my ear, "There was a time when you liked the two-bit whore."

I suddenly felt like an asshole knowing she was right.

But then her hands slid around my waist before they started to snake their way downward.

I stopped her hand before she could get a rise out of me, literally. "Tina, don't. You're drunk."

She pulled back and smirked. "So?" Her grin was inviting. Playful. Just the sort of look that would have lured me in a week ago.

"Go home, Tina. Before you do something you'll regret."

Her face shifted then as though realizing her ploy wasn't working. "The only thing I regret doing is you." A second later, she dumped my beer down my chest, much to the amusement of the patrons around me.

I knew the mature thing would be to let Tina walk away. She was drunk and angry, but I wasn't going to let her humiliate me like that. I needed to save face with the guys, so I reached out and grabbed her by the wrist before she got away. She let out a little shriek as I pulled her close to me.

"You and I both know you don't regret a single moment with me." My voice was hot and thick with insinuation. It was also a line. I knew we'd never had anything more than hot sex. But damn it all, I was sexually frustrated at the moment, and Tina might be the thing to get my mind off Sam. Sure, it meant reverting to my old playboy ways, but maybe that's the only way there was. Maybe trying to "grow up and settle down" wasn't in my DNA. Perhaps I was always meant to be a wild child.

Looking down at Tina, at the upward curve of her smile, I knew I was in. I could see it all play out. We'd go back to my place. We'd screw each other's brains out. I'd rehire her, and we'd continue to use each other to fill the void in our lives.

"Wanna get out of here?" I asked, already knowing her answer.

Her grin turned wide as she licked her lips. "What I want is for you to go to hell."

With that, she ripped her hand out of my hold and marched out of the bar.

"Son of a bitch," I muttered down at my wet shirt.

I was pissed. Not only because I was tired and soaked, but mostly I was angry at myself for being a dick to Tina. I deserved that beer down my shirt. And then some.

Annoyed at myself, I grabbed my coat off the chair. I was about to storm out when I noticed Joe was looking at me funny.

"What?" I asked. My voice was thick with agitation.

"That she…isn't you…much today."

Okay, I knew Joe was drunk, but even so, that sentence was gibberish.

"Cut the shit, Joe. I'm going home." The group around me was laughing and making fun of the situation but not Joe. There was something off about him. He kept mumbling something, but it was as though he was talking with only half of his face.

Warning bells went off in my head. I knelt down to become eye level with him. "Joe. Are you okay?"

"Then why she cave sometime around…" he said.

Huh? That made no sense. This wasn't like Joe. He was talking, but logic seemed to be missing.

My heart began to race. Something wasn't right.

"Joe." I shook my friend as something I'd read online popped into my head. "Joe, smile for me."

An odd grin spread across the man's face. A smile that only touched the left side of him.

"Jesus. Guys, I think Joe's had a stroke."

"Ah, she'd like to stroke it!" One of the men laughed. He was clearly too shit-faced to understand the seriousness of the situation.

Without thinking, I lifted Joe up to his feet, who was unsteady at best.

"Come on, Joe. We're going to the hospital. Now."

Even as I walked Joe to my car, I second-guessed myself. Maybe he was only wasted. Was I overreacting?

"No. Better to check," I whispered to myself.

It probably would have been smarter to call an ambulance, but I knew I could get him to the hospital faster. Our rinky-dink town only had one hospital and one ambulance. No telling if it was out on a call. The hospital was a short five-minute drive away. What little I did know about strokes was that time was of the utmost importance. If it was a stroke, Joe didn't have time to wait.

I had barely parked the car in the hospital lot when Joe took it upon himself to open his door, causing him to fall flat onto the ground.

"Joe! Jesus. Help! Help! Someone get me some help," I shouted toward the people in scrubs milling around on a break near the entrance. "I think he's had a stroke!"

Without another word, they came rushing over to help.

"What seems to be the problem?" a man in dark blue scrubs asked.

"He can't smile right and he's talking gibberish."

"All right, sir…what's his name?" the guy asked as a few others came over with a gurney across the lot.

"Joe. Joe Hewins. He was at a bar, having some drinks, and then he sort of started talking weird. He can't smile right," I said, rubbing my hands together to try to calm my nerves. "Are you a doctor? Is he going to be okay?"

"I'm a nurse," the man said. "But we're gonna get him some help. You did the right thing..." he said, searching for my name.

"Finn."

He took my hand and gave it a quick shake. "I'm Nurse Jacobs. We're going to bring him in and they'll run some tests and monitor his vitals. I need you to come in and do some paperwork. Can you do that?"

"Um, yeah, sure. Of course."

He reached out and gave my shoulder a reassuring squeeze. "It's going to be okay."

I nodded but saw the concern in his eyes. This was serious.

The other workers lifted Joe's two-hundred-fifty-pound frame onto the gurney with practiced ease. If I hadn't been so scared, I would have been impressed.

I followed after them toward the hospital as though I was going to be able to do some good once I got inside. In reality, there wasn't much I could do, except try to reach his wife.

Unfortunately, his wife, Maggie, was out of town at a business conference, but I was able to contact her on her cell. Maggie gave me the insurance information the hospital needed. She was a nervous wreck, so I stayed on the phone with her as she booked her flight back.

"Please," Maggie begged me before she hung up. "Please stay with him until I get there. I don't want him to be alone if he…" She couldn't even say the words.

"He's going to be fine, Maggie. He's being taken care of," I offered, knowing full well that didn't mean anything.

"Please, Finn." Her voice was thin with raw emotion.

I swallowed down the lump in my throat. Joe couldn't die. I wasn't ready to lose someone else. "Of course I'll wait," I promised.

And I did. For hours.

I paced in the empty waiting room, made a few calls, though not to Jackie. It was late, and I didn't want to wake the boys. There wasn't anything she could do anyway. I'd fill her in sometime in the morning after I had some clue what was going on. At the moment, no one seemed to have any information for a non-family member. It was beyond frustrating to not know what was happening. That's when I saw the nurse who helped us earlier walk into the waiting room.

"Nurse Jacobs?"

"Call me Scott," he replied, tossing me a scrub top. "I'm off now, but thought you if you were still here, you might wanna change out of that shirt. You kinda smell like a brewery."

I glanced down at my shirt, which was now almost dry but clearly still smelled.

"Hey, thanks." I took the proffered shirt and held it in my hands for a moment.

"You weren't drinking and driving, were you?" Scott asked.

"No! No," I said. "Honest, I spilled my beer."

Scott's eyes narrowed, trying to pull out the lie that was there.

I lifted my hands up in surrender. "Okay, I didn't spill it. It was spilled on me." I sighed. "I may have ticked off a chick I fired. She took her anger out on my shirt." I sighed, looking down at the mess.

Scott nodded. "Where do you work?"

"I own Must Love Coffee. The little café on the corner of Main and High street."

"Oh, right. Love that place. Great Americanos."

I smiled. "Thanks, man." I felt bad I didn't recognize the guy. Even in a tiny town like Bucksville, it was impossible to know everyone.

"Any word on my friend?"

Scott shook his head. "If there was, I wouldn't know about it unless he was giving birth."

"Come again?" I asked.

Scott laughed. "I'm a pediatric nurse. But they'll come in and update you when they know more."

I nodded in understanding. "Well, thanks for the shirt." A yawn rocked through me just then.

"There's a coffee machine in the hall. It's not as good as your place, but it will keep you up if you need it." Scott said, hooking his thumb over his shoulder.

"Right. Cool. Thanks."

As Scott left, I could feel my own exhaustion take over. I changed my shirt in the restroom, tucking my old shirt in my back pocket. Dry again, I made my way to the coffee machine in a feeble attempt to stay awake. I had a feeling this was going to be an epically long night.

As I fished out some change from my pocket, I stopped dead in my tracks at who I saw.

Chapter 8

Sam was here, at the hospital. Her back was to me, but I could see her profile walking beside an older man, maybe in his early seventies. Judging by his robe and the IV pole he leaned against, he was a patient. One hand had a firm grasp on the pole and the other was clutched around Sam's waist. He seemed to be walking with great difficulty.

It must be her father. He was clearly sick. That would explain why she'd been so distant. Her mind had been on an ailing father.

I had to turn away. I felt like I was intruding on a private moment, so I ducked behind the vending machine. Through the glass, however, I saw them continue to walk down the hall. They turned into a room a few feet away.

From my hiding spot, I could hear Sam talking, but I couldn't make out what she was saying. If I were a few feet closer, I bet I could make out some of it...

Curiosity got the better of me. I found myself moving out of my hiding spot and toward the room. Since Sam wasn't being forthcoming about her dad being sick, maybe I could find it out on my own.

"Well, that was a good walk, huh?" I heard Sam say. There were some sounds of what must have been him getting in the bed, so I risked a quick walk by the room to take a peek.

Sam was pulling the sheets over her father and kissed him on the top of his head. "I think you deserve that pudding." She turned then, catching my eyes. *Shit.*

I froze like a deer stuck in headlights. Too stunned to move and too embarrassed to speak.

Sam held my gaze but spoke to her father. "I'll be right back with that pudding."

Her dad's eyes were closed, clearly exhausted by the walk.

Flinching, I took a step back, trying to come up with a good reason for spying on her but coming up short.

"Finn? What the hell are you doing here?" she said in a whisper, pulling the door shut. "Are you following me?"

"What? No. I'm here with a friend."

Her eyes narrowed. She didn't believe me.

"Seriously. I think he had a stroke. I drove him in. I was going to get coffee when I saw you. I wanted to make sure it was you before I said 'hi.'"

Sam's face shifted, but her level of suspicion didn't waiver.

"Hi," I said weakly, lifting a hand up to wave.

She fought back a smile. "I'm sorry to hear about your friend."

I scratched at the back of my head before digging my hand into my jeans. I did that when I was nervous. "Yeah. It's kind of scary, actually. I'm waiting to hear. It's been forever and no word. I'm hoping no news is good news."

Sam gave me a small nod, but her mind was a million miles away.

"Sorry to hear about your dad." I gestured toward his room.

"That's not my father." She sighed. "It's my husband."

"Wait? That old gu—" The words had slipped out of my mouth unintentionally.

Instead of being offended, however, Sam only lowered her head, as though she was used to the ageist remark.

"He wasn't so old when I married him." Her voice was quiet. Drained. She looked as though she might collapse at any moment.

"I'm sorry. That was a jackass thing to say," I offered.

She shrugged and walked over to a row of chairs near the coffee machine and sank into one.

"I was young and clueless about the world when we met. And he was so smart and practical. He had both of his feet on the ground." Her eyes looked far off as she spoke. "I think that's what I fell in love with first: his passion and security in himself. I wanted that for myself."

I walked over to the seats as she talked and sat in a seat next to her and listened to whatever she wanted to say.

"It started out as a little flirting after class." Her eyes sparkled as she thought back. "Then, I started making up reasons to go to his office to discuss my paper, or my grades, whatever. Then it became this taboo thing that was new and exciting."

"Wait...Whitman...you married Professor Whitman? Our English professor?" My head whipped back toward the room. I was trying to place the features of her husband against the middle-aged man whose monotone voice had put me to sleep all those years ago.

She smiled. "Yeah. You didn't put that together?"

I blinked at my own stupidity. "Whitman is a common name…I guess I just didn't think—"

"That I'd marry an old guy?"

I flinched. "I did it again. I insulted you without meaning to."

She waved a weak hand. "It's okay. I'm too tired to care."

I sat there for a moment beside her, barely hearing the bustle of the hospital around us.

"What's wrong with him?" I finally asked.

Sam sat back in the chair and rested her head against the wall. She closed her eyes against the harsh glow of the fluorescents.

"Colon cancer."

Nodding, I leaned my head against the wall. "I have an uncle who had that," I said. "He's in remission now. They say it's one of the most treatable cancers if it's caught early."

Sam nodded. "And it's one of the deadliest if not." She closed her eyes for a moment. "Guess who had a stubborn husband who wouldn't get colonoscopies?"

"Ah," I said, for a lack of better words.

"The doctors tell us it's only a matter of time now before the cancer eats him alive." Her eyes began to well, but the tears stayed contained. "Today was the longest he'd been out of bed all week. One walk down the hall and he's completely drained." She shook her head. "The damn fool wanted to get out of his room. He wanted to walk on his own two feet…'one last time,' he said." That's when the tears broke free.

Her sobs were heavy and gut-wrenching, yet as silent as she could make them. No doubt she didn't want her husband to hear her mourning. It killed me seeing her in this much pain and knowing there was nothing I could do to make it better.

It was stupid, but I took her in my arms and held her. I couldn't help myself. It was the same reaction I had whenever my sister cried when she was hormonal during her pregnancy. It was the only thing I could think to do when I saw a woman cry. Sam didn't resist the embrace but rather sank into my arms as though she would have fallen to the ground if it had not been for my support.

After several minutes, her tears finally subsided. She pulled away from me and began to wipe her eyes. While I was glad she was no longer crying, I did feel an odd absence when she pulled away.

"Sorry about that. Wow. That's actually the first time I've cried about it," she sniffed. "I've been trying to stay strong, you know? For him."

"There's no shame in crying," I told her. "I'm sure he'd say the same thing."

Sam laughed and dabbed at her eyes again with her sleeve.

"Actually, he's begged me not to cry. He can't bear to see me upset. He told me I can cry all I want when he's dead." A few rogue tears escaped as she let out a shaky breath. "I love that man so much, as he loves me. It may seem gross to some people because he's so much older, but we genuinely do love each other. He's my life. My rock." Her eyes went across the room, lost in thought. "I don't know what I'm going to do without him."

I wanted to be able to offer her words of comfort, but the truth was I didn't know what to say. I'd lost both my parents suddenly, within a few months of each other. There was no time to say goodbye. And yet, I couldn't even imagine how hard it must be, knowing the end was coming and waiting for them to die. It had to be unbearable if Sam's emotional state was any indication.

"I hate that I have to work so much and be away from him," she said, wiping away the last tears. "But his medical bills are so high...our insurance, well, it isn't great. And then there'll be the funeral costs..." Her face crumpled. "I even feel bad sleeping. It's time I'm wasting. Time I could be with him." She shook her head then rubbed her temples. "I feel like a zombie. Only barely conscious. I don't know what I'm supposed to do."

I took her hand and gave it a squeeze. "Well, right now, in this moment, you're going back to your husband. You're going to pull up a chair beside him and close your eyes, holding his hand in yours. Like this," I said, gesturing to our hands, "so he can be with you, even in sleep."

She hung her head but nodded.

"In the morning, after you've rested, we can talk more. I can help. Even if it's only to pick up your groceries or water your plants. Heck, I have a good shoulder to cry on, too, if you need that again."

She smiled. "You do have a comfortable shoulder."

"It's the scrubs," I confessed. "They're super soft."

"Yeah, why are you wearing scrubs?"

Sighing, I took out the shirt from my back pocket and waved it at her. "That's a long story, but it involves a perfectly innocent bottle of beer."

"That sounds like a good story." She laughed softly. She stood up and straightened herself. "Okay. I'm going back in." She looked down at me. "Thank you, Finn."

I stood up and rubbed her shoulder. It was too intimate a thing to do, I realized, but I felt like we'd made a connection in her grief. "It's not a problem. Any time. That's what friends are for, right?"

She shook her head. "I wouldn't know about that. Ben is the only friend I have these days," she said, nodding toward her husband's room, "but thank you. You've been very kind to me tonight."

"Well, thank you. You've given me something to do other than worry about my friend."

"Oh my goodness. Here I've been blabbering away and you have a friend you need to go to." Her face was riddled with guilt.

"It's okay. They told me they wouldn't know anything for a while. They have a lot of tests to run. They told me to go home, but his wife asked me to stay until she got here, so here I sit, or rather, stand."

She reached out and touched my arm. "You're a good friend."

I hated how that simple sentence stung. Friend. That was all I'd be to her. It would have to be enough. She didn't have anything else to give. "Go. Be with your husband. The worry will still be there in the morning."

"That's for sure." She let out a breath. "I'm gonna go get him that pudding for when he wakes up."

"Great idea."

Sam smiled, as though relieved to have a plan, even if it was only walking to the cafeteria for gross pudding. She gave me a final nod before turning and heading down the hall. I kept watch over her until she disappeared down the stairs and even then I waited. I'd been shaken by the last few minutes and needed a moment to let my own reality slip back in.

"Sammy?" A weak voice came then from her husband's room. "Sammy?"

I looked down the hall, but Sam was long gone.

"Are you out there?" her husband's voice asked.

I stared at the door for a few seconds before I did something completely foolish and opened it.

 Chapter 9

The door closed behind me, giving an ominous *clink* as I took a few tentative steps inside. The room had the predictable sterile smell of bleach and artificial lemons. So clean yet so ripe with death. It was an olfactory conundrum. My shoes squeaked against the waxed linoleum as I shoved my hands deep into the pockets of my jeans.

"Well, you're not my wife," Mr. Whitman said with a small smile as I made my way farther into the darkened room. There was only a tiny glow of a small light near the bathroom to illuminate his face.

"Um. No, she went to get your pudding."

Mr. Whitman cocked his head to the side. "Are you my night nurse?"

I looked down at my scrub. "Oh, no. This isn't mine. Um. Something spilled all over my T-shirt. One of the nurses gave me this to change into," I said, realizing coming in here probably wasn't the smartest thing I'd done. "So, yeah, Sam will be right back. Did you need something until then? I could go find a nurse."

He sat up a bit in his bed. "No, I thought I heard her talking, is all." Mr. Whitman looked up at me and waved me closer, so I took a few more steps in. A wave of recognition washed over his face. "Ah. I thought so. You look well, Mr. Allen."

"Thanks. I can't believe you remember me."

The old man smiled. "I've got cancer, not dementia, Mr. Allen. I remember all of my students. Particularly, the ones who used to ogle my wife."

My eyes widened. "What? No, I never—"

"Oh, sure you did. All the boys did back then. It's okay."

Well, this conversation was not going well. "Look, no disrespect, to your wife, but she was a pain in the ass back then."

Mr. Whitman began to laugh at my crude joke. It took him a few minutes to recover from the exertion. "Yes, I suppose you're right," he finally agreed. "She was young and stubborn…"

"And arrogant and cocky and condescending," I added.

He nodded slowly with my assessment. "I suppose we've all changed a bit since then?" He raised his eyebrow up as though questioning my own less than perfect days.

"Touché," I concurred. "I don't want to interrupt your rest. I just wanted to make sure you didn't need anything. Sam will be back in just a few minutes." I started to back out of the room, ready to excuse myself from this awkward conversation.

"Would you mind terribly sitting with me until she gets back? I don't get many visitors these days," Mr. Whitman urged, gesturing to a nearby chair.

"Right. Um. Sure. Yeah, I can do that." I made my way nervously over to the chair to sit down beside a man I barely knew while we waited for my employee to return and question why I was even here.

"So, Finn. What brings you to my neck of the hospital?"

"Oh, um, a buddy of mine suffered a stroke. Or at least that's what I think it was. I'm waiting for his wife to show up in a few hours. They won't tell me anything since we're not blood related."

Mr. Whitman nodded. "Yes, they're a stickler for those sorts of things, aren't they?"

"Hardcore. Doesn't matter to them that Joe is like a father to me."

"Mmm." Sam's husband looked at me for a long moment. "I am relieved to hear you have a legitimate reason for being here. At first, I thought you might have come in with Sam."

"No. I was shocked as hell when I saw her here. I didn't even know you were sick."

He smiled. "Yes, Sam is a very private person. But you did know she was married?"

"Yes. Of course."

"Good." He adjusted his position again. He couldn't seem to get comfortable. "I suppose I let my mind wander a bit. I assumed you and Sam were, well, you know."

My eyes grew wide at his insinuation.

"It's not like that at all, Mr. Whitman. I promise you. She's a good worker, and I had a friend that was sick. That's it. Honest."

He gave me a small smile. "I believe you. To be clear, I wouldn't have been angry if she'd found someone to keep her company. Lord knows I haven't been a good companion these last few months." The hum of his monitors seemed to echo his statement. How awful it must be for him to be trapped in this room knowing the end was coming. "Tell me, Finn, does Sam have any girlfriends at your shop? Women she might confide in?"

"I-I'm not sure. She only just started. There really isn't anyone there her age, well, besides me, but I'm sure Sandy will warm up to her once she realizes Sam doesn't want her job."

"I worry about her, Finn. I worry about the seclusion she's put herself in. She used to be a social butterfly. When we lived in the city, she had girlfriends over for wine every week. They went to the movies, shopping, lunches. We used to tango every Tuesday...now all she does is work and sit with me. Doesn't seem like much of a life."

I wasn't sure if he was referring to Sam or himself in that particular moment.

"That's it," I whispered.

"What's it?" Ben asked.

I looked up, realizing I'd said that out loud. "Nothing. It's just...I saw Sam looking at a poster at the local Salsa Studio. I wondered if she liked to dance because—" I stopped myself before I could make myself look like an ass in front of her husband.

"Because what?"

Dammit. I was trapped.

"Because I was given couples salsa lessons for my birthday by my sister this year, as a joke because she loves to poke fun at my single status, and I was going to offer them up to Sam."

He nodded. "I'm afraid I wouldn't make a very good dance partner anymore."

"Yeah. They say it's a good stress reliever, though," I said, rambling about things I'd read on the brochure.

"I don't doubt that," Mr. Whitman agreed. His long, skinny fingers tugged at the thin, blue hospital sheets.

"What's going on here?" a voice said behind me.

I turned around and saw Sam standing there, a spoon in one hand and a vanilla pudding in the other.

Mr. Whitman lit up like a Christmas tree when she walked into the room. "I was talking to your employer, my sweet."

She walked and stood next to me, one eyebrow raised to the sky. "Yes, I can see that. But *why*?"

"Oh, we were simply having a talk. Man to man, you know?"

"No, actually, I don't know," Sam said in a tone that indicated she wasn't going to let the subject drop.

Her husband seemed to expect this reaction because he merely smiled. "Don't be mad, darling. I'm only trying to secure a partner for you."

She made a face. "A partner? For what? What's going on?" She faced me, a look of accusation in her eyes.

"Don't look at me. I have no idea what he's talking about," I said, standing up.

Mr. Whitman took his wife's hand and rubbed his thumb along the back of it.

"Calm down, peanut. I simply mean a dance partner."

Sam and I both looked at each other, bug-eyed.

"What?" we said at nearly the same time.

"Finn was just telling me he got salsa lessons for his birthday. He wanted to give them to you since you are such a fine dancer, but since I can't lead you out on the floor anymore, I thought perhaps Finn would do the honors."

Ben looked up at me as though I could provide some sort of backup, but there would be no backup for him throwing me under the bus like that.

"I swear, I have no idea what he's talking about," I said.

Sam looked back and forth between her husband and me.

"So you don't have salsa lessons you're trying to pawn off onto me?"

"No. I mean, yes, I have lessons, but I wasn't trying to insinuate that…" I was digging myself into a deeper hole, and I didn't know how I got in it in the first place.

"It would be good for you to get out of the hospital, my love. Do something fun for a change," Ben tried.

"I do have fun. With you," she cooed, resting her hand on the side of his face.

"I'm worried about you, Sam. You never take any time to practice self-care. You're wasting away before my very eyes. I long to see the spark of the girl I fell in love with. The one full of life and energy. You need to take some time for yourself and get out of this damn hospital," he said, his voice rising louder than I'd heard him speak. One of his monitors went off as a result.

"That's it. I'm calling the nurse. You need more morphine." Sam was in provider mode despite Ben's best attempts to keep the conversation going.

"Darling, please listen to me. I'm worried about you. You are retreating inward and it isn't healthy. You need to get out. Make some friends."

"Ben, but I don't need any friends. I have the best one in the world right here." She took his hand in hers and squeezed it.

"But for how long, my love? Even the doctors can't tell if it will be weeks or months. Now is the time to make plans. How can I be at ease if I don't know who will be there to help you when I'm gone?" Ben's strong voice began to waiver. As though fully understanding his limited time left. He was settling his affairs. Trying to make sure his most precious treasure was going to be given to a good home. It broke my heart to watch.

"You can't think like that," she pled.

"No, darling. It's you who can't accept that I'm going to die."

She stood up then and grabbed his plastic container of pudding and chucked it across the room where it barely missed me and splattered onto the floor in a great white blob.

"And so you asked Finn to take your place, is that it?" she shrieked.

"Whoa. I never said I was going to take your place," I said, looking at Mr. Whitman to help me out of this.

"Was this your idea?" She whipped around to glare at me. "First salsa lessons then, what? Dinner? The movies, a quick lay back at your place?" Her face was hot with anger, though even I could tell the anger wasn't directed at me but at the situation.

I raised my hands in surrender. "No! Sam, that's not it at all."

She turned her venom back onto her husband. I stood there like an idiot. Not knowing what else to do, I walked over and started to clean up the mess of the pudding using my beer soaked shirt.

"See, he's already being helpful," Mr. Whitman said with a sadness in his voice that hadn't been there before. "This is what I'm talking about, Sam. You need someone to help you through the tough times when I'm gone."

"I don't need a babysitter." Sam let out a huff. "Finn, stop cleaning the damn floor."

Holding back my own frustration at the situation, I stood up, leaving my rag of a T-shirt over the mess as though covering a dead body.

Ben looked up at his wife and outstretched his hand, which she readily took as she sat down beside him. The tension in the air melted away as Sam bent down and gave him a tender kiss.

I had to look away. I was an intruder on this very intimate conversation and it was high time I left. Quietly, I began to back out of the room as Mr. Whitman kept talking.

"My only regret in this life is that I won't be able to provide for you anymore. I won't be able to make you smile, or laugh. I'll never get to take you out to dinner, drink wine or dance in our living room until three in the morning..."

"Ben, we'll dance together again," his wife soothed through tears as I inched closer to the door, desperate to leave them in peace.

"Yes, my love, we shall. Just not in this life." His own voice was thick with emotion now. This must be so hard to do. He was so much stronger about his impending death than I ever would be.

He lifted Sam's head to look her in the eye.

"You have so much more time to dance, my love," he whispered. "I want you to. I need you to."

She shook her head hard. "You know I can't dance alone. I'm useless without a strong dance partner to guide me." She smiled, trying to lighten the mood.

My hand was on the door.

"I have the sore toes to prove it," her husband said, kissing the top of her head. "I know you don't believe in fate, but I believe the universe has handed us a gift in Mr. Allen. He has waltzed into my room with an empty dance card." Ben's tone indicated no trace of anger or sarcasm. "Go out, darling. Have a night off. "

"What? Ben, no. I'm not going to some stupid dance class with my boss when I could be with you. It's not happening."

"Peanut…please. For me? Make an old man happy."

"By dancing with another man?" she growled.

Ben laughed a bit but then had to cough a few times as a result.

"I'm not asking you to dance with Finn and fall madly in love with him, like you did when we first started dancing."

Sam's face blushed at the memory.

"I merely want to allow you some downtime. For your own sake, as well as my own, go out and dance. Forget about hospitals and my pending death and this god-awful smell of bleach. Hell, I bet Finn won't even mind if you step on his toes." Ben looked up, searching for my answer. What did he want me to say? This was all so confusing so I just blurted out the truth.

"My toes are crushed by my staff on a daily basis. I can't even feel them anymore," I said, tapping the toe of my sneaker on the floor for good measure.

Ben smiled as though that settled everything. "Now, when do those classes start?"

"Ben—" Sam began.

"Sunday night," I replied.

"Perfect!" He looked up at his wife. "You don't work on Sunday."

Sam brought her attention back to her husband.

"I know. I scheduled it that way. It's the one chance I have to be with you! I'm not giving that up and I'm not going dancing with anyone but you. Do you understand?" Her voice was strong. Unwavering.

Ben sighed and glanced over at me.

"I think we might need a moment alone, Finn."

I nodded, grabbing the door handle again.

"It's fine. Forget it. I shouldn't have come in. I need to check on my friend anyway. I'll see you at work."

I caught Sam's eyes and tried to convey in that brief exchange just how sorry I was for putting her in this position. She gave me a single nod, and I realized she was in the same boat as me. We were both adrift and lost, just in competently different seas.

Chapter 10

I left Ben's room, trying not to feel like I'd just been rejected. I mean, logically why *would* Sam want to leave her dying husband to dance with her boss, a man she barely knew? And yet, I still couldn't help but feel deflated.

Maybe it was just the whole situation and utter lack of sleep that had me feeling off. I needed a few minutes of shut-eye. A mental reset. Since I couldn't leave the hospital until Maggie got here, I opted to head to the waiting room and crash in one of the chairs for a few.

My plan was thwarted, however, when I walked back into the waiting room and found my sister there, pacing the room and biting her nails. Her thin brown hair fell down her shoulders, her trademark headband locking the strays firmly in place. It was the same hairstyle she'd had since grade school. While I liked to tease her about her relentless predictability, right now I needed someone as unwavering as her.

"Jackie!" I said with relief, despite my entire body sagging in exhaustion.

Her brown eyes flicked up at me as her lips curled into a smile.

"There you are. I thought you went home already. What's happening? How's Joe? No one will tell me anything because we're not freaking related."

My eyebrows shot up. "Freaking?" It wasn't like Jackie to use vulgar language and "freaking" was about as close as she got, and only when really angry.

"Yes, freaking," she repeated, although she lowered her voice to a whisper when she said it the second time. "They don't care that the man is like an uncle to us, or that he's at our house once a week for meals, or even that he carves our family's dang pumpkin each year…"

"Wow. A 'freaking' and a 'dang.' You really are pissed."

She gave me a quick punch to the arm that hurt more than she probably intended it to.

"Hey, what was that for?" I rubbed where she'd hit me. She might be small, but she was mighty.

"That was for not calling me earlier. I had to find out from my hungover husband that Joe was in the hospital."

"I thought you'd be in bed. Sheesh. I didn't want to wake you or the boys. Besides, it's not like there was anything you could do about it anyway. All I've done is call Maggie and wait for news myself."

She huffed and crossed her arms, not about to back down. "Yeah, well, you should have called me."

"I can see that now." I inspected my arm for a bruise.

"Hey, what's with the shirt?" Jackie asked looking at my scrub.

"It's not mine. One of the nurses lent me his. Mine was...dirty."

"Oh, yes. Nick mentioned something about some chick dumping her drink on you."

Her eyebrows pinched together in a judgmental frown. She knew there was a story there. One I was hoping not to tell anyone, let alone my sister.

I sank into a chair and rubbed my face a few times, knowing I was going to have to explain. "Yeah, that was Tina."

Jackie made a face. "The bimbo from the shop?"

"Yeah. I sort of fired her today. Guess she wasn't too happy about that."

"Ah. In that case, well done."

I nodded in agreement, intentionally leaving out the bit that I was intending on sleeping with her until she shot me down cold. I'd rather like to forget that slip in judgment.

"So you were with Joe at the bar? What happened?" Jackie was clearly more interested in Joe than Tina.

"Yeah, he'd bugged me to come down and shoot some darts. We hung out for like an hour, and everything seemed fine. Tina showed up pissed at me, so I decided to leave. When I was grabbing my jacket Joe said something garbled. I thought he was pulling my leg or something, but then his whole face looked weird."

"Like he was only using half of it?" Jackie asked.

"Yeah. How did you know?"

Jackie rubbed her hands over her face. "Nick's grandfather died of a stroke."

"That's right," I said, but I honestly hadn't remembered. Not that I paid much attention to Nick's side of the family. I tolerated him because I loved my sister but made no other effort than what I had to when it came to him. Nick was an asshole.

"Where's Maggie? She hasn't been picking up my calls." Jackie dug out her cell likely to check for any returned messages.

I leaned back in the chair. "Her phone is probably dead. She's flying back from Denver from a conference. She got the first flight she could but still, it's a long flight with a two-hour layover. I told her I'd wait for her until she got here." I lifted heavy eyes up to her. "She didn't want him to be alone."

Jackie nodded. "Right. And he won't be. I'm here now. You go home. Get some sleep." She made a face at me. "You look like a dog that's been beaten and left to rot."

"Gee, thanks." I laughed. I certainly felt like it. "You sure, though? What about the kids?"

Jackie rarely left the house past eight. Once the boys were in bed, she was in bed.

"Nick is home," she said, twirling her wedding ring absently. "Let me help. Please, I want to help. I need to do something."

The pleading in her eyes had me giving in. I was way too tired to put up much of a fight, anyway.

"Fine. Call me if you need me to take over."

She waved her hand. "Don't be silly. You have a shop to run."

I looked up at the clock and sighed. I still had a pile of work on my desk to finish. There was very little time off when you owned a shop. All of that could wait, though. Sleep could not.

I gave Jackie one final hug, easily engulfing her tiny body in my arms. I kissed her once on the head, then made my way back, finally, to my bed.

Naturally, once my head hit the pillow, I couldn't sleep. My mind kept drifting back to Sam…and the idea of feeling her hands on me on the dance floor. I felt like a complete asshole for thinking about her when I should have been worrying about Joe. I wrestled with the guilt of conflicting thoughts until I let my imagination take over and I drifted off into a tantalizing dream about a woman I could never have.

When my cell went off the next morning, I answered it without even looking at the number.

"Sam?"

"Um, no. It's Greg, man."

I frowned at myself. *Why had I assumed Sam would be calling me?*

"Right, sorry. What's up man?"

"I'm, like, totally sick." Greg was the only guy at the shop since Kenny left. He was a part-timer. The guy was forty-five and still lived with his mother. He only worked to pay for his pot habit. We had an understanding. As long as he didn't show up high, he'd have a job. He'd kept his word and had been one of my hardest workers for the last five years. He never called in sick, and by the sound of his voice, he wasn't faking.

"Flu?" I asked.

"I don't know, man. I've been hurling and shitting my pants all morning."

"Gross," I said. I didn't need to know the details. I dragged my naked ass out of bed and looked at the calendar of shifts stuck to my fridge. He was scheduled to be in from two to close.

"Right. Well, can't have you doing that on customers." I let out a huge yawn. "I'll cover your shift. Be well, man."

"Thanks." I hung up before he could tell me any more about his illness. Greg would talk your ear off if you let him. He was nice enough, but a lonely guy. Single. Starved for company. *Shit.* He was essentially me.

I jumped into the shower and downed a pot of coffee before I checked in on Joe. My sister sent a text to say that Maggie had arrived, so I opted to go for a quick visit before my shift. I grabbed a tray of coffees first from the shop and placed them precariously on the seat of my car.

When I arrived a few minutes later, the two of them were both talking with each other in the corner of the waiting room. Their voices were hushed, clearly not wanting to disturb the few other people waiting for news of their loved ones. Jackie's eyes lit up when she saw me.

"You brought real coffee!" she squealed.

"And here I thought you were happy to see me. You just want my goods. Story of my life," I joked. I got a light punch in the arm from Jackie, who grabbed a cup for her and one for Maggie.

"Thank you," she said. This time I could hear the genuineness of her gratitude.

"I'm surprised you're still here. Don't you need to get the kids off to school?" I asked, taking a sip.

"Nick's got them. He's not good with hospitals."

I nodded, remembering when the kids were born. Nick was green the entire time. I took a seat next to them. "So, how's Joe doing?"

Maggie lowered her cup. Her face was drawn and her eyes red, either from crying or lack of sleep. Probably both. Her wild gray curls were refusing to stay tucked behind her ear. She always exuded so much life and energy, but today she looked vacant. She let out a shaky breath. It was clear she was having a hard time trying to get the words out, so Jackie stepped in to help.

"Well, we found out it was a stroke. A TIA or something-or-other type of stroke."

My heart began to beat faster, fearing what the news would mean.

"They call it a mini-stroke, I guess. The doctor said she should be able to break up the clogged artery but only because you were so fast at bringing him in." Jackie gave me a thankful grin. "They think that much of the damage will be reversible. In time."

At that, Maggie spoke up, "He's going to need to learn how to talk again, though…to relearn some words his brain has wiped clean." There were tears in her eyes. "But he knew who I was. He remembered me." She gave me a huge smile. It seemed as that was the most important bit of information to relay. And perhaps it was. In Maggie's eyes, if her husband knew who she was, they could still connect in some way. If they had that, then it wouldn't matter what condition his speaking would be.

My stomach gave a loud growl, causing my face to redden.

"Oh, man. I guess I should have brought some muffins or bagels to go with these coffees." I rubbed my stomach in an effort to tame the beast.

"There's a cafeteria on the first floor," Jackie said with no trace of subtlety.

I nodded, standing up. "I'll get us an assortment."

Maggie looked up at me and smiled her thanks, and Jackie gave my hand a gentle squeeze of appreciation.

It felt good to be doing something other than stand around. It kept my mind busy which, considering the inappropriate places it wanted to wander last night, was probably a good thing.

Once there, I scanned the cafeteria, searching for sugary pastries to sustain us. When I passed the chip display I stopped short.

Sam was standing in line at the counter with a cup of coffee and something in a small brown bag.

My first instinct was to shout out her name. My second was to bolt before she saw me. I went with the latter and spun around with my still hot coffee in my hand and promptly crashed into the wall. My coffee spilled all over myself and onto the floor around me, causing a huge ruckus.

Naturally.

Chapter 11

I tried not to curse as the hot coffee ran down my stomach and into my jeans. I tried really hard. It didn't work.

"You can't seem to stop spilling stuff on yourself, can you?" Sam asked, approaching me with a handful of napkins.

I took the napkins for what little good they would do now that the java juice was embedded into the fibers of my clothes.

"What can I say? I'm a basket case," I muttered, pulling my T-shirt off my stomach to air it out.

Sam laughed at my feeble attempt to dry off. It felt good to hear her laugh, but she recovered quickly, almost as though she felt guilty for enjoying life for a moment. Shaking her head, she began dabbing at my shirt with the pile of napkins. Her hands were brushing against my chest in such a way that if the napkins were gone, it might be interpreted as the touch of a lover. Our eyes met as she seemed to realize the same thing.

"Sorry," she said, pulling herself away from me. "I guess I'm not used to people being able to take care of themselves." There was the faintest bit of blush appearing on her otherwise olive-colored skin.

"It's okay."

She turned her attention to cleaning the mess still on the floor while I wiped down the coffee from my forearm. I couldn't help but watch her work on the floor. I tried being careful not to look at her cleavage, though from my angle I had a damn good view. Damn good.

When we'd cleaned it up the best we could without a mop, Sam picked up her coffee and bag from the table to leave.

"Wait," I said, noticing the paper cup.

Sam turned around and I swear I saw a flash of hope in her eyes. "Is that *coffee* in your hand?" I gave her a wicked grin she frowned at.

"No. Cocoa. I needed the caffeine boost. I'm not sleeping great these days." Her eyes focused on her cup.

Uncomfortable with the sudden shift in the mood, I began to tug at my shirt again.

Sam laughed and grabbed my elbow. "Come on. I'll get you something to change into."

"Oh, no, it's fine. I think this might be my new look. Stained shirt guy." I grimaced at the lameness of my own joke.

"Don't be silly, you're soaking wet." She leaned in and sniffed. "And reek of coffee."

I laughed despite the insult.

"You look about Ben's size," she said, eyeing me. "Well, before he lost a lot of weight anyway, but I think I might have something that fits. Follow me."

I knew I shouldn't have, but I did. I'd likely follow her off a cliff if she asked me to. This was not good.

Sam made her way back through the labyrinth of the hospital without a single missed turn.

"How long has he been in the hospital?" I asked as we cleared yet another corner.

She sighed. "On and off for the last three months." She stopped walking and just stared blankly ahead of her. "How many more times do I have left to walk down this hall? To turn into his room and see him still struggling to smile up at me?" Sam reached out and touched the wall beside her. She looked like she was about to pass out. Without blinking, I was at her side, holding her up until I could guide her into a nearby chair.

"I just don't know what I'm going to do without him, Finn. He's my life. The only reason I wake up in the morning." Her tears began to fall.

I grabbed the cocoa and bag out of her hands and set them on the chair beside us.

"He can still be the reason you wake up in the morning, even if he passes, you know?" I offered.

She smiled. "It's not an 'if' it's a 'when.'"

I nodded. "Sure, but that can be said for any of us. None of us know when our last day will be."

Sam didn't say anything as she locked her eyes on a spot on the floor.

"When I lost my parents," I said, "I didn't have any time to prepare for it. They died unexpectedly within a few months of each other, but I think I felt very much like you do right now." I struggled to get the words out. I didn't like talking about their deaths, but I wanted Sam to know she wasn't alone. "I spent a lot of time in my room at their house...a house that was empty without them." I shook my head. "It's kind of pathetic, actually. I was in my thirties and still living in my parents' house. I was useless before their deaths and became a slug after it. I didn't want to eat. I didn't want to wake up. I didn't see the point."

Her hand pressed gently on my knee.

"I think I can relate to that part," she whispered.

I let out a breath. "Then one day, I woke up and decided enough was enough. I put their house on the market and moved into the office area where they kept their old files above the shop. Took about a year, but I converted that space into a pretty kick-ass bachelor pad."

Sam grinned. "I bet it's fabulous."

I shrugged. "I thought so too, ten years ago. Now? A man my age shouldn't still be living in a bachelor pad. He should be married, have kids..." I shook my head and looked down at the floor. "I'll always regret that my parents didn't live to see the man I should have been." My eyes flicked back at Sam. "They only got to see the self-absorbed jerk you knew in college. I was the guy who didn't care about anyone except the next chick I was going to bang." I flinched. "Sorry, that was crude."

"No, it was honest."

"I guess." I wasn't sure why I was telling her all this. Something about her made me want to reveal all my secrets.

"So, you took over their shop?" Sam asked.

I was fully aware of the fact her hand hadn't left my leg.

"I inherited it. At first, I wanted nothing to do with it, so for a while, my sister, Jackie ran it. She was great at it, but she hated being away from her boys. They were so little then. She gave me a stern lecture, reminding me that our folks left the shop to me. Not her." I frowned. "I never understood why they did that."

Sam smiled. "Because they believed in you. They saw your potential for greatness even when you couldn't."

I scoffed. "There's nothing great about what I've done with my life. I've wasted it. I have nothing to show for it."

"And neither will I once Ben is gone," she whispered and then began to sob.

I pulled her into my chest and let her cry. This form of grief I couldn't relate to as I didn't have a chance to prepare myself for their deaths. What she was going through had to be a million times worse. I didn't blame her for the tears but wanted nothing more than to wipe them away.

"Of course you will," I soothed. "You have years filled with memories. Nothing can take that from you. Not even death." Her head bobbed up and down on my chest as the tears flowed. "That's what I eventually realized with my folks. Sure, they weren't physically with me anymore, but they were always with me, in here," I said, pointing to my head. "I still talk to them sometimes. When I'm having a hard time or if something amazing happened. I pretend they're still with me and, I don't know. It makes me feel better, I guess. It feels like they can hear me."

Her hand clutched onto my shirt and her breathing calmed. It really didn't matter what I said, I realized. She only needed someone to hold her. Someone to tell her everything was going to be okay. I was more than happy to be that someone.

"It's going to be okay, Sam. You'll get through this. It's going to be okay."

"I want to believe you, Finn," she whispered. "More than anything."

"Shh." I lowered my lips to her head without thinking. I stopped myself just short of kissing her head even though every bone in my body wanted me to. I had to be her friend, not her lover. She already had one of those. "We're both going to be okay," I said more for myself than for her.

Chapter 12

I held her in my arms like it was the most natural thing in the world to do. It felt right, which was wrong. I was allowing myself to partake in a fantasy world where we ended up together. It was dangerous and reckless and yet, I couldn't seem to pull myself away.

"Finn? What the heck is going on?" Jackie's judgmental voice came from behind, a figurative yanking of a child by the ear when caught misbehaving. It was a tone she reserved for when she was disappointed in me. I was quite used to it by now.

Sam pulled away at her question, leaving my chest cold and hollow. I glared at Jackie, who was too busy sizing up Sam to notice.

"I'm sorry," Sam said. "I wasn't flirting with your guy, honest." She stood up and grabbed her things, rushing to be free of this awkward situation.

"No. We're not together. Sam, this is my sister, Jackie Abbey."

Jackie didn't ease up on her eye-lock on Sam.

"Oh?"

I swear I saw a flicker of relief on Sam's face for a fraction of a second.

"Nice to meet you." Sam extended her hand, but Jackie didn't take it. She looked down at her outstretched hand, then turned her focus on me.

"I went down to find you in the cafeteria in case you had your hands full." She glanced at Sam. "Guess I was right."

"Knock it off, Jackie," I bit back. It was one thing to call me out on my womanizing tendencies, but it was another to insinuate Sam was just another one of my conquests.

Sam seemed to pick up on my anger as she defused the situation.

"Oh, no. It's not like that. I'm here visiting my husband. He's dying and, well, I'm not taking that news so well." Her eyes filled with tears. "Finn was kind enough to provide some comfort, that's all." She looked back at me. "Thank you, again."

She gave me a small smile, then disappeared into her husband's room.

"Well, that was awkward," Jackie said, sitting where Sam had been. "Didn't mean to break up that love connection."

"Jesus, Jackie. It's not like that, all right?"

Jackie cocked her head. "Whoa, easy, killer. I was just making conversation."

I stood up and turned my back on her. "No, you weren't. You were making assumptions. Again. I can be friends with a woman and not want to bang her, you know?"

"Okay, fine. Sheesh. I didn't mean to offend."

Calming down, I walked back over and sat down beside her. "It's fine. I guess I'm protective of her. She's going through a lot right now. I don't want to add to her stress."

"Right. Who is she? And why is your shirt wet *again*?"

Closing my eyes, I ran my hands over my face. "That's Sam. She's the woman I hired when Kenny left. And nothing happened with my shirt. I'm just a klutz and spilled my coffee."

"Ah." She looked back down the hall where Sam had disappeared from. "She's not your usual type."

"Jackie, I told you. It's not like that. She's married." That didn't seem to placate her.

"To a dying man, by the sounds of it." She pursed her lips in a knowing way.

"Jackie. Stop. I know what you're trying to do, so just stop. There is nothing going on between me and Sam."

As though on cue, Sam appeared in the hall. She was walking toward me, fast. My heart leaped at the sight. I got up and rushed over to her.

"What is it? Is it Ben?" I asked, searching her eyes for answers.

Sam's face flushed for the briefest of moments. "No. He's fine, still sleeping." She held up a white T-shirt. "I forgot I was going to give this to you."

I looked down at the shirt. "Oh, right. Thanks. You didn't need to do that. I would have been fine. It's almost dry now."

"Yes, but you still stink," she said as if that should settle the matter.

I laughed as she held out the shirt. "Right. Thanks."

Sam gave me a small smile. "You're welcome." Our eyes lingered on each other a moment until Jackie cleared her throat.

"I should get back." Sam gave me a final grin, then left back down the hallway as I yanked my old shirt off and put on the new one.

Jackie was frowning as I pulled my head through the T-shirt.

"What?" I asked.

"She's into you."

I scoffed. "No, she isn't. She's used to helping people, that's all."

Jackie's eyes were locked on where Sam had left.

"I guess she was helping herself to the gun show, too."

I made a face. "The gun show? What the hell are you talking about?"

"She watched you, Finn. She watched from the end of the hall as you took off your shirt."

I whipped around to peer at the now empty hall.

"She did?"

"Yup." The sound of her "p" echoed off the walls.

"She's into you," Jackie warned. "The fact that her husband is sick makes this so much worse."

"Jackie, you're overreacting."

She grabbed my elbow and yanked me hard to face her.

"This isn't a joke, Finn. She's an emotional mess right now, dealing with a very sick husband. She doesn't need your 'wham, bam, thank you, ma'am' antics."

My mouth opened in shock at her words. "Wow, Jackie. Just...wow. My own sister thinks I'm only good for a one-night stand."

I yanked out of her grasp and stormed off.

"Finn, that's not what I meant, and you know it."

"Isn't it, though?" I said, without turning around. I was fuming. Not at Jackie if I was honest, but at myself for realizing she was right. I wouldn't be good for Sam or anyone for that matter. I was a player. I always had been and I always would be. It was stupid of me to try to be her friend. I couldn't do that with chicks. It wasn't my style.

I dug my cell out and called the shop to let Rebecca know I'd be covering Greg's shift, but that I'd be a little late. I was spiraling down a dark train of thoughts and there was only one place that could get me out of it. I needed to talk to my parents.

It was odd, but I talked to them when my life felt like it was floundering, which was a lot these days. And yet, I hadn't been to their gravesite. Something about seeing their names on the stone made their deaths permanent, and as long as I didn't see it, it wasn't real. It was foolish, I realized, but it was something my mind hung onto. The time had come, however. The time for childish head games was over.

While I'd never actually been to the site, I knew exactly where it was. We lived in a small town. One cemetery held us all, and I'd been to the family plot plenty of times to put flowers on Grampa's stone on Memorial Day. The rectangle of land where the Allen Family would be permanently laid to rest was both ominous and sacred.

"Come on, Finn. You can do this," I chided myself once I got out of the car. The lot was empty save for an elderly woman near the front. I forced my feet forward to talk to my folks.

When I reached their joint headstone, the first thing I noticed was the pale salmon color. It stood out among the depressing shades of gray surrounding me. While I knew that was the color Jackie had picked out for them, it was a shade they would have enjoyed. An apt reflection of the color they brought into our boring lives.

I kneeled down to trace the deep etching of their names, ignoring the chill of the ground against my knees. The grass had not been mowed and had begun to lose its bright hues while brown leaves clung to the corners of their stone, seeming to seek escape from the late autumn wind for a moment.

"Hey, Mom. Hey, Dad," I whispered. "Sorry I haven't been around much, or well…at all." I glanced over my shoulder to check if there were any other people within earshot before I went on. "I have no idea what I'm doing here." I tugged at the wilted grass around me, intermittently tearing out blades and tossing them away as I spoke.

"Let's see. Um, I'm still at the coffee shop, much to my dismay. I sold the house like you wanted. Got a good price for it. All your debts are taken care of. Jackie put her money from the sale toward the kids' college fund. I still don't know what to do with mine. I don't really have anything worth spending it on, I guess."

I was racking my brain for things to say to them. It felt foolish talking to them in the past tense.

"But you probably know all of that, don't you?" I peered down at the stones. "You're watching over us, I bet? Looking down at your grandkids as they grow up? Observing your son flailing around like he always did? I guess some things never change."

The wind kicked up and loosened a few of the leaves, turning them into wild circles before they came to rest again at a new stone.

"I met a girl..." My hand ran over my face as though to wipe away the shame. "Don't get the wrong idea. She's a woman I work with. She's amazing. You would have loved her. She's beautiful, smart, funny, and off the market. Figures, huh? But I think meeting her was the Universe's way of kicking me in the ass. I've been thinking about this all wrong. When I met Sam, I thought she was going to be the woman to finally break me out of my old habits, you know? Show me the way sort of thing? But now...maybe Sam isn't the turn signal pointing me in the right direction but more of a stop sign. Maybe Sam showed up to remind me there's nothing for me in Bucksville."

That was it. It all made perfect sense now. Sam was here to save me from myself.

I stood up and brushed my pants off. "Wow. I know what I need to do now." I looked up at the sky absently as though looking for confirmation there. "It's time for me to move on. Give the shop to Jackie, or sell it. I don't care. I need to leave town. Start over someplace new where my baggage won't follow me. Guess that's what I've been saving that money for." I looked down at the stone. "It's not like there's anything keeping me here."

I paused where I was, waiting for the universe to send me some sign. Some signal to defy what I had said, but nothing came. Even the wind seemed to stop as not to give me any false hope.

"Right. I guess that settles it. I'll see you when I see you."

I left the cemetery with a sense of purpose. Yes, things needed to be done before I could leave, but at least there was an endgame now. There was a great sense of relief in that. It was high time I grew up and moved on with my damned life.

Chapter 13

When I finally made it back to the shop, my brain was foggy. I felt robotic as I took orders, made change, and prepared to close up for the night. If Rebecca noticed, she had the kindness not to say anything.

Sandy had likely warned her to leave me alone when I got like this. It didn't happen as much anymore, but there were some years I was an asshole to be around. Sandy was sure I didn't forget it, either. But she wasn't here and my ego was wounded. So what if I was a little broody. I suddenly felt trapped by the town I'd called home all my life. Now, I was biding my time until I could escape the small town hell.

It was clear to me now this wasn't the place for me. I couldn't live in a town where everyone knew my business and thought they knew who I was and what was best for me. No one knew the real me. Hell, not even my own sister. She was just like the rest. It wouldn't matter how long I stayed here or how much I tried to change. This town would always see me as the player I'd been in college. There was no escape from my past here. The only way out was to get out.

While I was anxious to leave, I was sane enough to realize I couldn't just cut and run. I was an adult. I had adult responsibilities that my younger self would have given the middle finger to.

Of course, the transition would take time. I needed to pack, find a new place to live, and, naturally, a new job...

Do I even know how to write a résumé?

The first step would be talking to Jackie about handing over the shop to her, even though I know she wouldn't want it. I at least had to ask before putting it on the market. I couldn't do that now, though. I was still too pissed at her to have a civil conversation.

When the shop's phone rang again I caught Rebecca's eye.

"If that's my sister, you can tell her where to stick her apologies."

Rebecca sighed and went to answer what was sure to be the umpteenth call from Jackie. She'd been relentless. First calling my cell but then trying the shop after I'd turned my phone off. Did she really expect me to pick up? She'd all but called me a whore. Then again, maybe she was right.

When we hit a lull, I sent Rebecca home early and tactfully shooed out the lingering couple who thought they could use the shop's couch as a make-out spot. Normally I wouldn't mind, but today they just ticked me off. Go be blissfully happy somewhere else.

There were still three hours left till close time, but screw it. I was the owner. I could close early if I wanted to. It was one of the only damn perks of the job.

I hurried through the closing tasks and ten minutes later, I was flicking off the lights and locking the door behind me. A bottle of Jack would help slip me into the numbness I craved. I could start looking for work someplace far away from here in the morning. Or afternoon, depending on how sloshed I ended up getting.

In my mind, I was already upstairs pouring my first drink, so when I turned away from the shop and crashed smackdab into someone outside, I almost hauled off and punched them. Until I saw who it was.

"Sam?"

Her eyes were downcast, and her hands were wrapped tightly around her body, as though trying to keep herself from falling apart. She lifted her head. Her eyes were red and puffy.

"Oh, my God, has Ben—"

She shook her head. "No. Not yet." She wiped her face. "Can we talk for a minute?"

"Right, sure. Of course. We could go into the shop, or do you need a drink?" I searched her eyes to try to find what would be of more help but saw only tears. "It looks like you could use a drink."

She let out a small laugh. "Yeah, I could use ten."

"Okay. We can do that. There are a few bars—"

Sam made a face. "I can't go anywhere looking like this."

"No. Right. Of course not." A bad idea popped into my head. "My place is just upstairs." I pointed upward to the row of windows above the shop. "I have whiskey, bourbon, vodka, and beer. If you want something else, I'll go grab it…"

She looked up toward my apartment, then back down at me. Her expression said it all. She was conflicted.

"Just drinks," I assured her. "And a friendly ear." I crossed my fingers over my heart, a gesture I hadn't done since I was a kid. "I promise. I'll even spill a drink on myself if that will help."

She laughed and nodded a few times in thanks.

"A drink and company would be great," she whispered. I could tell she was about to cry again.

"Right this way, then."

I shimmied my way around her to open the outside door that led up the one flight to my place. It was a narrow staircase that was only wide enough for one.

"I'm right at the top," I said, gesturing to the red door and fishing my key out of the stubborn lock behind me.

As Sam climbed ahead of me I tried my best to avoid looking at her ass, but it was impossible not to notice. It was literally right in front of my face...so round and lush—*Stop it, Finn. This is exactly what Jackie was talking about.* I had to focus. She needed a friend, and a friend was what I was going to be.

When she got to the top of the stairs she bit her bottom lip ever so slightly. Jesus. This was not going to be easy. The landing in front of my door wasn't much wider than the stairs, which meant our bodies were practically pressed against each other while I tried to find the right key to unlock my apartment. I clenched my jaw to force my thoughts elsewhere other than on her body against my back and ultimately pushed my front door open with more force that was necessary.

Flicking on the lights, I groaned. My face flooded with embarrassment at the condition of my apartment.

I looked around and saw my place for the dump she must have seen it as. There was a futon for a couch, leftover takeout containers everywhere, empty beer bottles perched precariously on mismatched end tables, and trash overflowing in the kitchen. It was the sort of apartment you'd expect from a college kid, not a man in his forties.

"Um, so yeah, I don't entertain often," I said, picking up empty pizza boxes and as many beer bottles as I could manage.

"Don't tidy up on my account. It's actually a relief not to be in a place that hasn't been bleached clean."

"Well, in that case…" I released all the trash I was holding to the floor. It garnered the laugh I was hoping to pull out of her.

"Please, sit." I pushed aside the dirty laundry on the futon so she could.

She hovered in the doorway for a moment before she came all the way in and sank onto the couch.

"What can I get you?"

"Whiskey sounds great, thank you."

"On it." I rushed into the kitchen, which was open into the living room. The sink was piled high with dirty dishes, which made me worried if I had any clean glasses left. A quick look in the cupboards revealed only a random assortment of coffee cups. Screw it. I grabbed the two closest to me. An "I heart Hulk" mug and one I'd stolen from the shop. I poured three fingers worth of whiskey into each. It seemed like we could both use the indulgence after our collective days.

"Okay, which one do you want?" I asked, coming into the room.

She smirked. "The Hulk, naturally."

That made me happy for some odd reason. I handed her the mug and sat next to her, being mindful to keep my distance.

Sam took a hearty sip and sat staring at the cup for a few minutes before she spoke.

"Ben's blood work came back today...it's not good. We'd been hoping he'd get the full six months they predicted, but his blood counts aren't good. They are moving him into hospice care in the morning."

I sat there, not sure what I was supposed to say.

"It's supposed to be more comfortable there," she continued. "Better accommodations, round-the-clock care, and pain management." She took another drink. "But it also means there's nothing left they can do. It's where he'll go to die."

I wanted to say I was sorry, to try and say something to make her pain go away, but I sensed she just needed to talk. She needed to release the pent-up feelings inside her, so I kept quiet and let her vent.

"I mean, we knew this was coming. All the doctors had prepared us for this same outcome, but it's just so soon. Ben and I...well, *I* thought there would be more time." She broke down, and I couldn't hold off any longer. I slid over to her and took her into my arms. I stroked her hair and her back gently as she crumbled beneath me.

"It's okay," I whispered into her hair. "Everything will be okay."

Her tears slowed and she pulled away gently.

"Will it?" she sniffed. She didn't sound convinced as she reached for her mug and downed the rest of her drink. I followed suit.

She let out a slow breath and cleared her throat. "The reason I came to find you was not to break down like this, believe it or not. It was to ask you for a favor."

"Anything."

"Don't be so quick to say yes. I was wondering if you'd be willing to come with me tomorrow to the hospice."

"Of course."

Sam frowned. "Let me finish. You haven't heard why I'm asking you to come yet."

I cocked my head, confused. I'd assumed she needed some moral support.

"Okay...why do you want me there?"

She paused for a moment to study her glass, searching for the words.

"Ben asked for you to come," she said finally.

"Oh. Um, why?"

"The bastard won't tell me. He said that was between the two of you." Sam turned to look at me. "I'm hoping he's going to tell you he's taken back his request that you take me to salsa lessons in light of his faster than anticipated decline. I've told him I don't want to leave his side, especially now. I can't focus on anything but him right now."

"Sure, that makes sense," I said. "And I agree with you about the dancing. You absolutely need to be with him now."

"I'm going to have to quit my other jobs. Not yours, though," she said quickly. "I still need the money from all three but can't be away from him that long. And your shop...well, that's the one job I like. It's the one where I don't have to think about my husband nonstop because my mind is busy and surrounded by people, you know? The cleaning and the mail room are solitary. I'm with my thoughts as I work and lately, they have been consuming me. It's not a good place to be." She looked up at me. "In my head, I mean."

I knew all too well what being alone with your thoughts could do. "You don't have to worry about any of that now. There will be time to think about money and work, but it sure as hell doesn't need to be tonight. Tonight you don't have to think about anything at all if you don't want to."

I reached down and picked up the bottle of whiskey and poured us another round.

She gave me a shaky smile. "Thank you. That means a lot to me." After she dabbed her eyes, she continued. "Sorry. I've been a bit of a mess these last few weeks." She rubbed her face. "I can't sleep for more than a few hours at a time. I eat only whatever is leftover on my husband's tray, and even then it's not because I'm hungry, so much as I want the nurses to think he's eating better than he is." Her breath shook. "He didn't want to have to rely on a feeding tube. He wanted to keep some level of dignity."

I reached out and took her hand, giving it a gentle squeeze. "You're a good wife. He's lucky to have you."

Her bottom lip trembled, and I knew more tears were coming.

"Hey, look. I'll be there tomorrow. No problem, okay? For now, how about we just talk a bit? Tell me about Ben. Tell me all of the things you love about him."

And with that, we slipped into easy conversation. She told me about their first dates, their wedding, and honeymoon. It was bizarre. She was sharing these very personal and intimate details about her life, but neither one of us seemed to realize we were essentially perfect strangers. I felt as though I'd known Sam my entire life. Talking with her was so easy. It was like breathing, and I couldn't get enough.

For hours I sat and listened to her stories. The funny ones and the sad. The fact that Ben had to resort to being an adjunct professor shocked me the most. I didn't know there was a difference.

"Wait…you're telling me that adjunct professors don't get healthcare?"

Sam shook her head. "Nope. He's considered part-time so no health insurance, no retirement, no nothing."

"Jesus."

She changed subjects either because she saw I was upset or she didn't want to think about it herself. It didn't matter what we talked about. I just liked listening.

It wasn't easy to hear about Ben's early days getting sick, but the miscarriages she'd suffered were worse. I spoke little, only asking a clarifying question here or there. It was helping her to talk about the better days with her husband. I could see the shift in her posture. This was calming her senses, and I didn't want to screw it up. So, I ordered some pizza, and we continued to talk in an effortless manner while managing to polish off the rest of the bottle.

"And what about you, Finn?" a now very tipsy Sam asked. "Who was your first love?'

I laughed, finishing off the crust of my pizza and tossing it onto the paper plate where it slid off and fell to the floor.

"I'll let you know when it happens."

Sam sat up, slipping her legs off my lap where they'd somehow ended up resting during the night.

"Shut up. You've never been in love?" The way her voice sounded, so shocked and filled with pity made me feel like shit.

"Now don't misunderstand me. I've been with women. A lot of women. It's just…" I stood up to pour another drink, but sort of hovered in the middle of my living room, too drunk to remember why I got up. "None of those women held my attention for longer than a night." I shrugged. "And I certainly would have never stayed up until four o'clock in the morning shooting the shit with any of them."

Sam glanced up at the clock.

"Oh, God. It's so late. We have to be at the hospital at nine for Ben's transfer." She stood up too, very wobbly. "Shit. I'm so wasted. I got to go."

I shook my head vehemently. It made my head spin. "No driving for you."

"I walked," she said as though that settled everything.

"Well, I'm not letting you walk at this hour, either. You'll sleep with me."

Sam snorted.

"No. That came out wrong." I chuckled with her. "You can crash in my room. I'll take the lumpy old futon."

"I'll be fine," Sam said as she took a step and nearly fell over. "On second thought, maybe a bed is a good idea."

I took her hand casually, and she didn't resist as I brought her into the bedroom. I ripped back the sheets and let her fall into bed. She rolled over to the right-hand side of the bed, leaving a nice and inviting spot for me.

"I always sleep on the right," she murmured before closing her eyes.

"That's fine. I always sleep on the left."

I turned the light out, fully intending to go back to the living room. But the room began to spin just then, so I sat down to steady myself. I had no intention of lying down beside her...let alone falling asleep. Honest.

Chapter 14

I knew I was dreaming because reality had never been so amazing. It had been a long time since I'd fantasized about a woman in my bed this hot, so I tried my best to hang onto the dream for as long as I possibly could.

In this current fantasy, I was lying beside a woman who was on her stomach, naked as the day she was born. Her golden skin shimmered in the morning light, and I found myself unable to resist touching her.

My lips found the nape of her neck where I planted a few delicate kisses. Her soft moan indicated her enjoyment, so my lips traveled farther down her back, following the slight curve of her spine. She rocked toward my lips as my hands found the woman's lush ass. Man, was I a sucker for a good ass, and this woman had that and then some.

My hands latched onto her hips, turning her over gently so I could see this vision in all her glory. She gave into my demand to roll over. Her eyes were still closed, but a smile was etched on her beautiful lips. Jesus. Never in my life had I seen a more perfect woman. Unable to stop myself, one hand reached up to latch onto her breast—

"Um, Finn?"

That's when I woke up.

My eyes flew open and saw a very confused Sam. It took me a few more agonizing seconds to realize I hadn't been dreaming at all and I was, in fact, cupping her breast. Under her shirt. Full skin to skin contact.

"Oh, my God." I pulled my hand away and stared at it as though it had committed a crime, because I had. I'd touched her without consent. My stomach rolled. "I'm so sorry. I-I was having a dream."

My eyes were still locked on her breasts as she ripped the covers up and over her. "A really good dream, apparently," I said, taking in the bulge in my jeans.

"Did we—" she asked, clutching the sheet tighter around body.

"No," came my immediate reply. "At least, I don't think so." My head began to throb. Hard. I flinched against the pain. "I mean, we still have our clothes on, so I'd think not."

Sam let out a breath and nodded to herself. She was clearly relieved that she hadn't betrayed her husband, well, aside from sleeping next to her boss and having had him manhandle her.

"I'm going to take a cold shower," I said needing to distance myself from her. "After, I'll whip us up something to eat. I think we could both use something a little more solid in our stomachs."

Sam glanced at the clock radio beside the bed and shook her head.

"We can't eat. We have to be at there in thirty minutes."

I nodded toward the shower. "I only need two."

She smirked at the unintended innuendo.

"I meant in the *shower*. The shower will only take me two minutes. I can last more than two minutes in bed. Way longer."

Her smirk turned into a full-out laugh. It was nice to see. That is until she grimaced.

"Ow. I shouldn't be laughing." She felt her head with the hand not holding her sheet. "It hurts."

"Yes, it does. I've got some aspirin in the medicine cabinet." I headed toward the bathroom, but she stopped me with an outstretched arm.

"Hey, Finn." She tugged a bit harder at her blankets. "Can this stay between the two of us? Whatever the hell happened, that is?"

"Oh, sure. Of course. Never happened."

She gave me a silent nod, almost as though she were disappointed with my answer. Or maybe that's just what I wanted to believe. I was reading into things. I had to get my head out of the clouds. She needed emotional support, not someone who was going to grope her in her sleep.

The drive to see Ben was little different. We sat as far apart as the car would allow, and all eye contact seemed to be banned, which was fine by me. I was still horrified with myself. I'd touched her without her consent. Alcohol or not, that was unforgivable.

"Ready?" I asked as I parked the car, eager to get this nightmare over.

"No," Sam admitted. "My head is still throbbing, my eyes are bloodshot, and my body is still on fire from this morning."

"On fire?" I asked, confused by her meaning.

She swiveled in her seat and looked at me.

"Don't take this the wrong way, okay, but waking up that way, with your hands on me—it got me stirred up." She lifted a finger. "Not because it was *you* fondling my breast, it's just...it's been a long time." She lowered her head. "It's been months, actually."

I sat in silence as she looked out the window.

"I don't blame him for being sick and not being able to have sex. I mean, there isn't a lot of privacy at the hospital, you know? And even before then, in between doctor's visits and research into new treatments, his exhaustion coupled with my own, and the constant cleaning up of bloody stools...it hasn't exactly left the door open for intimacy."

"Right. No. I get it."

She shook her head, indicating I really didn't understand her.

"Sam, trust me. I do get it. You're not into me. Got that message loud and clear." I stared at the steering wheel. "Look, can we just never bring this up again." Did she have any idea how humiliating this was for me? How big of an ego blow it was?

"Finn, don't take this the wrong way, but I don't think we should hang out anymore. In fact, I should probably quit." Her voice dropped.

Turning to face her, I noticed her conflicted expression.

"Do I repulse you so much that you actually have to quit your job just to be away from me?"

Her eyes widened. "No! No, that's not it."

"So what is it then?"

"Look, it's just that…I love my husband, without fail—"

"I know that," I interjected. I was well aware of that fact.

"But being close to you isn't a good idea. It's sending my brain mixed signals."

"Mixed signals?" What the hell was she talking about?

She was growing more and more flustered. "I'm just saying that after you speak to Ben and hear whatever the hell he's planning on telling you, I need you to keep your distance. Okay?"

At first I thought she was joking, but there was some legitimate fear behind her eyes. I knew I'd crossed a line last night, but her current reaction seemed a bit too extreme for my subconscious mistake.

"Wait a second. You think because I had one drunken dream, I won't be able to keep my hands off you? Is that it?"

"No." She sighed. "It's the other way around." Instead of explaining her comment, she got out of the car and walked into the building.

I stared at the door she'd disappeared into the building through, leaving me in complete and utter confusion. She was worried that if we continued to hang out, *she'd* grope *me*? Was that what she'd just said? Did that mean she liked me? Or did it mean she hated me for turning her on when she was in love with someone else?

Cursing, I hit the steering wheel. "Why are women so damn confusing?"

Obviously, I'd need to get to the bottom of this, but now was not the time. Adjusting my glasses, I got out of the car and jogged to catch up to Sam. The sooner this was done, the sooner I'd be able to figure out what the hell just happened.

When I made it inside Sam was already talking to one of the nurses. She was a stick of a woman with her hair pulled back into a severe bun, but she still managed to have a kind face.

"Sorry I'm late," I said, walking up to Sam, trying to make it appear as though we'd come here separately. Sam seemed to appreciate the gesture.

"It's okay. I just got here myself."

The nurse looked up from her computer screen and walked with us to Ben's room. "I'm Nurse Littlefield. I'll be his day nurse this week. There's a whiteboard in his room that will let you know who will be on each week, but you'll catch on soon enough."

Sam nodded as we rounded a corner.

"How is he doing? He didn't want me here until he was settled in, stubborn fool." She muttered the last bit under her breath.

Nurse Littlefield didn't seem fazed. "That's understandable. It's really a rather boring process. A quick ambulance ride. You didn't miss much."

"I don't want to miss anything," Sam said, twisting her hands.

"Understood," the nurse said. "On a positive note, he seems to be in good spirits today. He's tired from the move over, but he was still smiling when I gave him his pain meds."

The nurse stopped in front of a door. Sam looked up at it, and I could see the color drain out of her face.

"This is the room he's going to die in," Sam whispered.

I longed to assure her that wasn't true, but I couldn't.

"Mrs. Whitman," Nurse Littlefield said gently, breaking the tension. "Remember, there are no visiting hours here. Stay as long as you need. The chair next to his bed pulls out to a twin mattress. It's not the most comfortable thing, but it serves the purpose well enough."

Sam nodded. "Thank you." Her voice was strained. I wanted to reach out and hold her. I wanted to tell her she wasn't alone, that I'd stick with her through all of it, despite her desire to keep our distance. But this was not my place to speak. Instead, I hung back as the third wheel in a life that wasn't mine.

Chapter 15

Sam went inside Ben's room as I paced in the hall waiting for her signal to come in. To see her husband. How was I going to look him in the eye knowing what I had just done to his wife? *What was I even doing here?* This felt wrong. I didn't belong here.

Through the door an argument between them broke out. While I couldn't hear what was being said, I could make out the anger in Sam's voice. Something had set her off and as much as I wanted to help her off the ledge, I knew it wasn't my place. Shaking my head, I stood up to leave.

That's when Ben's door whipped open, halting my escape. Sam was standing there with her hand tight on the handle. Her face was red with anger. Anger that appeared to be directed at me.

"He wants to talk to you." She sent a glare in the direction of her husband before she turned back to me.

"Sam, what's going on?" I asked, taking a timid step forward.

"I don't know what to say to him. I'm so angry." She took a few breaths before she returned her attention to me. "Maybe you can help him see logic because I can't seem to!" She threw her hands into the air for a moment and then regained her composure. "Go talk to him. I need to go find out when the doctor will be here. Clearly, his meds are off."

She brushed past me, shoving me with her shoulder as she did. I watched her storm down the hall, wondering what the hell her husband had said to set her off like that.

"Don't mind her. She'll cool off in a moment," Ben's frail voice said from inside.

"Morning, Mr. Whitman." I swallowed down my nerves and went into the room.

"Call me Ben, please."

My eyes widened at his new digs. It looked more like a bedroom than a hospital room. Dark blue wallpaper with gold accents lined the walls. They matched the deep velvet blue curtains, which had been drawn back with gold tassels. It was a very masculine feeling room. A stark contrast to the bleached white walls of the hospital. Even the bed looked like a regular bed in some respects. It had a down comforter with some decorative pillows. The floors, though covered with a thick wax, looked like real wood, but I doubted they were. It was quite cozy despite the bank of monitors and gadgets behind his bed.

"Nice place you got here," I said, gesturing around.

Ben chuckled. "Isn't it, though? People are just dying to get in."

I tried to laugh at the bad joke, but my heart wasn't in it. Ben didn't seem to mind.

"Sam sounded pretty miffed." I slid a chair up to him.

Ben nodded a few times. "Yes, I would say she is."

"Everything okay?" I knew it was none of my business, but I asked anyway.

"It will be. Once she's come to terms with it."

"Your death?" I asked, realizing a second too late how crude that was.

Ben laughed, regardless. "No, I'm not sure she'll ever come to terms with that one." Ben's long, aged fingers ran across his covers, smoothing out creases that weren't there. "No, she's angry with me because I asked her to do something for me. A final request, if you will."

"Oh?"

Ben nodded sagely. "Yes. I knew it would be a difficult request, and I'm actually relieved she's so upset about it." He smiled at me. "It proves how much she loves me."

"She does, you know. She loves you, like, a lot." I was embarrassed by my juvenile choice of words.

He smiled brighter. "I believe you. And I believe her when she tells me as such, but she's still young. Well, younger than I am, anyway. I've had a bit longer to ponder things than she has, you see?"

I nodded like I knew where he was going with this conversation when I hadn't a clue.

"When I die"—Ben looked up at the ceiling absently— "I shall leave Sam with a huge financial burden, some of which my life insurance will cover, but not all of it." He turned to look at me. "You know she's been working three jobs because of me?"

"Um, yeah. I do."

"It won't be enough," he said. "She's keeping her head above water as it is. Even with insurance, the medical costs will be a burden. Once I'm gone, there will be little left for her to live on."

He looked out the window then as though searching for his words to be etched somewhere on the glass. "I've taken care of what affairs I can on my end, but it's after that time that worries me, Finn."

I was still confused. I knew Sam was worried about the money. I would be too. "Look, if you're thinking I'm going to fire Sam for taking time off to be with you, I've already let her know her job would be safe. There's no rush for her to come back. Whenever she's ready."

Ben's eyes closed for a moment. "Well, that's very kind of you, but I was thinking of more than her job security."

"Okay..." I said, trying to follow the train of thought he wanted me to pick up on.

"My wife is strong. One of the strongest women I know."

I nodded in agreement.

"But she's also stubborn and emotional. She'd scold me to call her such, but she is. She feels things so much deeper than I do. Her compassion is one of her greatest qualities but also one of her weaknesses."

"I can see that," I agreed.

"Although she's tough as nails, she's also a person who needs human connection. She does not do well on her own."

"I'm not sure any of us do," I said honestly.

"I'm glad to hear you say that," Ben said. His voice was weaker than the last time I'd seen him. In fact, every bit of him seemed weaker. His energy was struggling to keep up with the words he seemed determined to let out. "I have to ask you a question, Finn. Well, maybe a few, if you don't mind? They will be personal questions, but I'm dying and there's no time for tact."

I sat up, uncomfortable. "Um. Okay. Fire away."

"First, are you currently dating anyone?"

My eyebrows shot up. Was he serious? The frown Ben gave me indicated he was. "No...why?"

Ben nodded, ignoring me. "Second question. Are you healthy?"

"Um, yes, I think so," I answered, my confusion escalating.

"Don't skip your physicals. Do you hear me? Get your colon checked. Don't be pig-headed, like me, and think you're immortal. Go and let them run all the tests on you that they want to, understood?"

I sat there, nodding, not wanting to make his condition worse by arguing with him.

"Third question. Are you attracted to my wife?"

I stood up. "What? Sir—Ben, no, it's not like that. She's a great girl—woman, but I'm not trying to steal her away from you if that's what you're asking."

Ben was very calm. "It's not. I'm asking, merely, if you think my wife is attractive."

I felt my face redden, giving me away.

"That's what I thought," Ben said with a small smile. "I would have been offended if you had said otherwise. After all, she's a beautiful woman."

"That she is," I said under my breath.

Ben pushed a button on his bed to bring him further upright. "That brings me to my last question. When I'm gone, when she has had the chance to mourn me, would you look out for her?"

"Of course. Absolutely," I said without hesitation.

"I don't think you understand my meaning. I'm not asking you to drop by now and again and play bridge with her. I'm asking, would you marry her?" Ben's white, bushy eyebrow lifted in anticipation of my answer.

I stared at him, waiting for the punch line. When he didn't speak, I tried to clarify his meaning.

"You want me to marry your wife?" I said, trying to wrap my head around the question. It made no sense, so clearly I was missing his meaning.

"Well, after I'm dead, but yes. That is the question."

I now understood why Sam was so upset. "Um, I don't think—"

"No, I don't want you to think, I want you to answer. I want to know if you will take care of my wife after I'm gone. I need to know she'll have a roof over her head. Food on the table. Arms to hold her at night. She needs all of those things. She deserves them, and Lord knows I can't do it anymore."

I stared at him, not sure what he wanted me to say.

"It's clear you fancy her and I have a sneaking feeling you two would be sexually compatible."

My eyes grew wide. "Sir, I haven't had sex with your wife." *At least, not that I can remember.*

"Ah, but you have touched her breast."

I felt all the color drain out of me. "She told you that?"

Ben smiled and rested his head back against his pillow as though happy to have it confirmed. "We have no secrets. Although, to be fair, I may have pried it out of her."

I opened my mouth to speak, but no words came out.

"I know her horny face, Finn." He coughed a few times and struggled to compose himself. "I know that face quite well, and I know for certain I wasn't the one to bring that shade of red to her cheeks this morning."

This conversation wasn't happening. This had to be a nightmare. I had to sit down to stop the room from spinning. "It was an accident, honest."

Ben laughed. "Oh, I know. I would have likely done the same in your condition. She *is* hard to resist. You should know she can't handle her liquor as well as she thinks she can, so do try and be careful in the future."

"In the future?" I blurted. "There isn't going to be a repeat performance of that. I was drunk. I thought I was dreaming with some other random chick." At that, I hung my head. "Trust me, Ben. You don't want me looking out for Sam. I can't even look out for myself."

Ben let out a small chuckle. "I was like that at your age."

I glanced up at him. His eyes were far away, lost in some memory playing only for him.

"Before I met Sam...well, let's just say that if the same laws we have now were in play as when I was a younger professor, I would have lost my job many times over for all of the indecent relations I had with students."

My eyebrows shot up at that thought.

"Back then," Ben went on, "I wasn't so much older than my students, only a handful of years, in the grand scheme of things. And all of the professors were doing it back then. You didn't brag about it, of course, but it wasn't a secret either." He sighed at the thought. "Women would throw themselves at you in those days, you know?"

I nodded. "I do, actually."

Ben raised an eyebrow.

"I used to play lead guitar in a band."

"So you *do* know." We shared a laugh and then Ben grew quiet. "Sam changed all that for me. From the moment she walked into my class I knew she was going to be in my life forever." He shook his head. "I can't explain it. There was something about her that had me wanting to say goodbye to my past ways. I began to wonder if bouncing from bed to bed was really the life I wanted to lead. For the first time in my life, I actually contemplated settling down."

Ben looked over at me. "You're nodding along with me," he noted. "She's had that effect on you as well, hasn't she?"

I couldn't answer him. While Sam had definitely turned my head, I'd been trying to settle down for a few years now.

Sam hadn't motivated that desire to find someone to share my life with, and yet, I couldn't deny that something changed when I met Sam. Some shift had occurred. I was no longer searching for just anyone to settle down with. I was searching for her.

When I looked back over at Ben, he was grinning like the Cheshire cat. "I see I chose her future husband well?"

Shaking my head, I stood up.

"With all due respect, Ben, she doesn't feel the same way for me. So my offering to marry her will do little good when she turns me down cold."

Ben flashed that same sage smile. "She may surprise you there." He let out a sudden moaning noise before pressing a button beside him.

"You okay?" I asked.

"I'm fine. Though you may want to step out for a bit, my boy. What the nurses are about to do here is a bloody mess of a job." Ben's eyes flicked below his waist, indicating his bowel area.

"Right. Sure. I'll go try to find Sam."

"Yes. Please. Try and convince her I'm only pursuing this because I love her." He winced again, clearly in pain now.

"You *have* met your wife, right?"

Ben nodded with a pained smile, as a nurse came in.

I took that as my cue to leave.

The door closed behind me, and I just stood there in the hallway for a few minutes, trying to process what just happened. He wanted me to marry his wife. It was a ridiculous question to ask of someone. Insane even. So why was I even considering it?

My forehead began to sweat. I needed air. This was madness. I wasn't going to force her hand in anything, let alone marriage. And yet, I couldn't stand the thought of her being on her own. She still needed a friend. I could watch over her. Even if it was from afar and would never be close enough.

"I'm judging by the color of your skin that my husband told you his crazy plan?"

I spun around at the sound of Sam's voice at my side. She was there, in the garden, sitting on a nearby bench.

"Um, yeah. He told me."

"Please tell me you told him how utterly ridiculous he is?"

I walked over to her and sat beside her.

"I actually didn't get around to answering him. He had the nurse come in."

That changed her sour expression. "Is he okay?"

"I think it was a bathroom issue."

Her face relaxed a bit. "They probably need to change out his ostomy bag."

I nodded but then admitted I had no idea what that was.

"He can't control his bowels anymore. So the bag takes care of the waste."

I made an unintentional face.

"Yeah, I know. Nothing about this illness has been pretty."

I reached out and squeezed her hand. "I'm sorry."

Sam looked down at our hands a moment before she pulled out of my grasp as she stood up.

"Come on, let's go inside. It's freaking freezing out," she said, shivering.

"What are you talking about? It's gorgeous out here."

She snorted. "Maybe for you, but I'm from Miami. I'm cold all the time."

I fought the urge to wrap my arms around her to warm her but, instead, relented and went inside.

Sam went to check on Ben. I wasn't sure if I should take that opportunity to leave or if I should wait to see how Sam was. I didn't know what my role in her life was at the moment and it felt odd to leave without knowing where we stood.

A moment later, she came out and sat in one of the chairs in the hall.

"He's asleep."

I nodded.

"He'll be out for a while. His pain meds make him tired." She rubbed at her face, exhaustion etched on it. "You should go—" She stopped in mid-sentence. "Wait, what day is it?"

"Thursday," I said. "No. Friday."

We both looked at each other.

"Shit!"

"I was supposed to open," Sam said.

"So was I," I chided myself. There was little to be done about it now. "It's fine. Be with your husband. I'll go in and tend to the shop and find coverage for your shifts."

"But—"

"No buts," I said, placing my hands on her shoulders. "Your place is here. With your husband."

Sam's eyes teared over at my words, but her face grew strong. She nodded once then left down the hall to be with the love of her life. It would be wise for me to remember where her heart was, and where it wasn't.

Chapter 16

The drive back to the coffee shop left my brain spinning. It was one thing to consider taking Ben's wife out dancing so she could get out and enjoy life for a moment, but it was a whole different story to consider taking over his role as her husband. Add to that mix a potential for sexual tension between Sam and me, and it had my thoughts all jumbled up. Did she want me to take Ben up on his offer? Or not? I couldn't be sure, and that was taking me to new levels of confusion.

I had to clear my mind of it. I needed to focus on the shop. I'd already missed the morning rush due to the fact that Sam and I weren't there to open up. Clearly, my head had not been focused the last few days. I needed to get a grip on reality. Maybe then, things would make sense.

After pulling into the back lot behind the store, I got out and rushed around the side of the building, anticipating a line when I got to the door, or at the very least, an irate note taped to the glass. But to my surprise, there was no line, no note. Instead, the lights were on and customers were inside.

"What the hell?"

Ripping the door open, I almost lost my shit when I saw who was behind the counter.

Tina.

Her silver nose ring glistened under the lights. Her black, choppy hair was lifted off her face in a large cloth headband. I stood there, perplexed. One, why was she finally in a uniform now that she was fired? And two, how did she get into the locked store that she no longer had a key to?

"You gonna stand there gawking all day or are you going to help?" a voice called out from behind.

"Kenny?" There he was, in the flesh, my best ever barista, bussing the tables.

"Glad you could make it in." He glanced intentionally down at his watch.

"What's going on?" I asked.

Kenny grabbed another empty mug off the table but nodded to my office. "When you didn't show up for work, Mrs. Abbey called us in."

"My sister called you?" I glanced back at Kenny, who nodded to the back room. "Excuse me a moment."

When I got to the office, Jackie was there, on the phone, talking in her firm "Mom" voice.

"I understand that, Donald, but you need to understand that your rate is higher than others. I'm going to be recommending to the management that they retain another vendor for their cream unless you can meet us halfway."

My eyes bugged out as Jackie held the phone away from her head, looking annoyed.

"They hung up on me. Can you believe it? Guess they didn't like hearing the truth."

"Jackie," I said, flabbergasted. "What the hell are you doing?"

Jackie stood up to try to meet my height. Even with her boots on, she barely reached my nose. That didn't diminish the fierceness of her glare. "Saving your ass," she barked.

I blew out a breath and closed the door to have this talk in private.

"All right, fine, yes. Sam was supposed to open with me today, but—"

"But you were too busy banging her to show up on time. Yes, I know."

My anger began to show now. She had no right.

"Get your head out of the gutter. That's not even close to what happened, but thank you for continuing to think so little of me."

Jackie crossed her arms in front of her.

"Oh, just drop the innocent act, Finn. Tina saw the two of you go upstairs to your room last night. She said you two looked awfully cozy."

"Tina said? What? Is she spying on me now?"

Jackie rolled her eyes. "Don't be stupid. She was coming to ask for her job back, you moron."

"So she told my sister that I was having an affair? Jesus, Jackie. I'm a grown man. I can make my own choices about who I bring to my apartment. It's none of your damn businesses what I do, or don't do, with Sam! And it sure as hell isn't Tina's!"

Her jaw hardened. "When you jeopardize the shop it becomes my problem."

I scoffed. "Jeopardize? The shop was only closed for a few hours. I think the people will survive. And it's *my* shop, Jackie. I do with it whatever I want to!"

Jackie narrowed her eyes, trying to figure out where my head was. Good luck with that.

"You're right. This isn't my business. I was worried, okay? You haven't been acting like yourself lately. You haven't even come to visit Joe since he's been in recovery. Not once! Hell, you haven't come to see your nephews in weeks. Now you're not showing up to work… I don't know what's going on with you." Her eyes widened. "Is it drugs? Are you on the drugs now?"

I rolled my eyes at how she said *the* drugs. "No. Jackie. I'm not a drug addict." I rubbed my hands over my face and sat. She was right. I was being a spaz lately. "I don't know what to say. Things are a bit of a mess now."

"You think?" she asked, her voice laced with sarcasm. "I begged Kenny to come back today only, as a favor to you, though I really think you need to hire him back. He's great."

"Yeah, I know he's great," I laughed. "That's why it sucked when he left for a better paying job that had benefits I can't afford to give him."

Jackie tapped her fingers on my desk. "Well, if you didn't use a payroll service, switched out a few vendors for local ones, and made a few of the items you sell yourself, you'd save some money. Maybe enough to hire him and Tina back. I've crunched the numbers and it could work…" Jackie had always been good with math. She had wanted to be an accountant, but then she had kids and all her dreams went out the window.

"I can't do the payroll myself. I have no idea how to do that stuff."

She shrugged. "I do."

"Well, I can't bake for shit, either, so that's out. Look, I have a system, Jackie."

"One that's barely keeping your business afloat."

She walked over and leaned against the desk. The thin legs wiggled under her weight.

"Finn, let me help you. I have lots of retired friends who love to bake and have idle hands who are longing for something to do. Plus, I know that Goose Farms must have a better dairy rate than what you're paying... I could make a few calls."

I gave her a sideways glance. She'd never taken an interest in the shop before. Why now?

"Fine, make some calls if it will make you feel better, but I'm not hiring Tina back. She hates me."

"No, she doesn't, Finn. She's desperate. She needs a job."

I scoffed. "Why, so she can get another tattoo?"

Jackie let out a measured breath. "She's pregnant."

My head popped up, trying to remember the last time we'd had sex.

"Relax, Romeo. It's not yours. I asked."

Relief flooded me.

"But she needs a job, now more than ever. She doesn't think the father is gonna hang around once he finds out, and she's scared out of her mind." Jackie glanced at the door for a moment. "She's a kid, Finn. You have to help her get on her feet. It's not her fault your cock got in the way of her working for you."

"Wait? What? How is this my fault? She's the one who didn't want to be here. If she did, she would have shown up on time, she would have worn the uniform—"

"Please, you know she never wore that because it would hide her tits from you." Jackie frowned.

"She pursued me, you know?" I said weakly. Not that it mattered. I knew exactly where she was headed with her lecture.

"You're a middle-aged man, Finn. She's twenty-seven. You should have known better. She doesn't know jack shit about what she wants. You're the adult. You should have kept it in your pants."

"Yeah, well, I just can't seem to do that, can I?" I said, recalling our last conversation. "After all, it's all I'm good for."

Jackie flinched at the reminder of her earlier attack on me but went on anyway.

"I'm only holding a mirror up to your behavior, Finn. It's your pattern. See a pretty girl, screw her, dump her, and find the next one. I mean, look at Sam. It's starting all over. What's worse, you blew off your business because of some chick you're banging."

I stood up, beyond frustrated with her attack. "She's not some chick, and I am *not* sleeping with her."

Jackie raised an eyebrow. "She just had a sleepover then?"

I let out a breath. "Yes, she came over last night. She was depressed. Her husband was being moved into hospice care. That's where they send you to die, Jackie," I said, making sure she picked up on the sarcasm. The way she looked down at the ground indicated she got the point. "She needed a drink and a shoulder to cry on. She was devastated. I couldn't send her away."

"So you just talked to her? All night?" she asked as though still unable to believe it.

"Yes. That's all we did. I poured the shots and she talked about her husband: how they met, how in love they were—are," I corrected myself. "She's a wreck right now, Jackie. An absolute wreck. The love of her life is dying in front of her eyes and I don't know how to help her deal with that."

Jackie nodded, either because she understood, or perhaps because she had seen this same thing with Maggie and Joe.

"She got shit-faced and I couldn't send her home like that, so she crashed at my place. Then, in the morning, she asked if I'd come with her when they moved him over to hospice care. She said her husband wanted to ask me something, but I also sensed she didn't want to go alone, you know?"

"So you were a shoulder to cry on?" Jackie asked, her tone far less accusatory now.

"Yes."

"And she slept where?"

My face turned red.

"My bed. I was going to sleep on the futon."

Jackie's eyes narrowed. "*Was?*"

I swallowed and looked nervously at my feet.

"Finnegan Nathanial Allen, where did you sleep last night?"

I paced a few times before I answered her. "I slept beside her. But not on purpose!"

Jackie's mouth flew open to accuse me of my old ways, but I stopped her.

"No. It's not what you think. We were both shit-faced. I helped her to the bed and then was going to go back to the futon, hand to God, but I sat down for a second and then the next thing I knew, it was morning…and my hand was on her breast."

Jackie sat there for a few minutes, her hands over her face in a mix of shock and horror.

"I was having a dream, I think… I honestly don't know how it happened. We were still dressed, so I know we didn't…but she totally had to wake me up to stop me from groping her."

The giggle that escaped Jackie's mouth conveyed the exact level of embarrassed horror I was currently experiencing.

"Oh. Wow. That's, well…that's something," she babbled. "What happened after that?"

"Well, we promised we'd never mention it again and then we had to leave for Ben's transfer." I shook my head. "I wasn't even thinking about the shop when we left, obviously. It wasn't on my radar, though I literally had to walk past it to get to my car. How pathetic is that?"

Jackie shrugged her shoulders. "Sleep deprivation mixed with a hangover and regret don't equate to logical thought."

"No," I agreed. "No, it does not."

Jackie scooted closer. "So what did the husband want? To tell you to back off his wife?"

I winced. Jackie noticed, so there was no way to get out of telling her the truth. "Actually, just the opposite."

"The opposite? I don't follow."

Rubbing my hand behind my neck, I let the bomb drop.

"He wants me to marry her."

When her jaw came off the floor, I backtracked a bit and gave her the shorthand version of the last few days.

"Jesus," she whistled. "No wonder you've been so out of it lately. What are you going to do?"

"Tell him no, obviously. It's not what Sam wants."

"Well, no. Of course not. Her husband is dying. The last thing she wants to think about is marrying someone else."

Jackie seemed to mull over her next words carefully. "What do you want, Finn?"

I scoffed. "It doesn't matter what I want."

"It does to me."

I sat with the question for a moment and tried to give her the most honest answer I could. "I want to be there for her in any capacity I can. But I'm not going to force her to marry me. That's insane. If I'm forever in the friend zone with her, then so be it."

"Oh, my God," she whispered. Her eyes were wide.

"What?"

"My little brother has finally fallen in love."

I wanted to protest, but the words refused to come.

Chapter 17

As Jackie waited for my denial of my love for Sam, I tried to reconcile my feelings for her. I mean, sure, from the moment I saw her I was taken aback, but she was beautiful. That didn't mean anything. Yes, she was easy to talk to and there was a certain feeling of comfort when I was near her, but again, that could be a bond of friendship. Just because I'd never had a female friend I didn't sleep with didn't mean friendship-only relationships were outside the realm of possibility.

Then again, waking to her in my bed, comforting her when she was upset, wanting to share my own thoughts with her. Thinking of her the second I woke up, searching for her in every room I entered, that was all new to me.

Maybe that was love, or at least the beginnings of it? I ached to hold her, to bring her comfort, to shield her from all pain. Did that extend to replacing her husband when he died? Was that to be my lot in life? A rebound? A rebound she didn't even want. A heaviness reached me, and my shoulders slumped. My eyes focused on the floor.

"Finn, answer me. Do you love this girl?"

"It doesn't matter if I do or not." I sighed.

She loved her husband and always would. Anything she felt for me could only be purely sexual. For once, that didn't interest me. I wanted more. I knew I'd just told Jackie I'd be happy with the friend zone, but the more I thought about it, the more I knew that would rip me in two.

"Why don't you take the rest of the day off? You look like you could use some sleep," she suggested. "I've got the shop covered."

I nodded. "I know you do. You were always the more business-minded of the two of us." I smiled at her. "That's why I'm leaving you to run it. Indefinitely."

Her face shifted from shock to anger as I walked over to the door. I opened it to leave, but Jackie blocked my retreat with her body.

"Finn, what's going on? What are you talking about?"

"I'm done, Jackie. I've failed. I see that now. I'm not doing anyone any good here. It's time I broke out of my same patterns. Like you said. I'm leaving the shop in your very capable hands and by morning, I'll be long gone. You won't have to worry about your screwup brother anymore."

"You're running away? Seriously?"

Breathing slowly as not to lose my cool, I placed my hands gently on her shoulders. "I'm not running away from anything. I'm just starting over. If I stay here, my life is going to go on exactly the way it is. I'll sleep my way through the town yet again, only this time I'll have to do it knowing that the only woman I want by my side is out of reach. I can't live like that, Jackie."

She looked up at me with her sympathetic eyes, and it felt like a knife to my heart.

"I thought I could. I thought just being her friend would be enough, but, damn it, I can't stop thinking about her. If I stay here, the most I could hope for from her is a friendly smile... I can't do that, Jackie. I'll go out of my mind." I pinched the bridge of my nose to keep the tears that pricked my eyes from forming. "Look, just promise me you won't fire Sam. She needs this job just as much as Tina does."

Before she could try to change my mind, I firmed my grip on her shoulders and lifted her easily off the floor to move her out of the way.

I could hear her screaming at me to stop, but it fell on deaf ears. I'd made up my mind. I was getting out of dodge while the getting was good. This would be better for Sam, too. She didn't need me around muddying up her grieving processes.

As I ran up the stairs to my apartment, it dawned on me I was probably having a mid-life crisis, but I didn't care. Nothing seemed more important to me than getting out of this stupid town. I'd live off the inheritance my folks left me. There was plenty there to start over. I should have done it years ago. Life in Bucksville was always going to be a dead end.

Once inside my apartment, I found a duffle bag in my closet and dumped some clothes inside. The rest I could replace whenever I landed someplace. Behind me, a door slammed. Jackie was there and she was fuming.

"You are the dumbest, most thick-headed, self-centered jackass I know," Jackie spat. Her face was red with rage.

"I happen to agree with you," I said, continuing to put things in my bag, "which is why I'm leaving."

I tried to brush past her, but she reached her hand out, grabbing me by the elbow, and pulled me back, hard.

"Whoa, easy there, killer," I said, taking my arm out of her grasp.

"No. You don't get to walk out on this, on me, and least of all on her."

I scoffed. "Who? Sam? She doesn't give a rat's ass about me. I'm a thorn in her side, a distraction from her husband in his final days. Trust me. It's better for everyone if I'm not around to screw things up."

She barred my way again with her body, and I arched an eyebrow as a reminder of how easily I could just pluck her out of my way again.

"Okay, the pity party ends now." Jackie grabbed the bag from off my shoulder and tossed it to the ground. "You aren't screwing things up. You're just scared."

I rolled my eyes. She was always trying to psychoanalyze me. "Oh yeah? Of what?"

Jackie's tone shifted from anger to sincerity.

"Of risking your heart. You're terrified of what would happen if you did."

"You don't know what you're talking about," I said, but my shoulders slumped, giving me away. That was exactly what I was afraid of. Sam had the power to destroy me. How could I stay and willingly let her do it?

Jackie stood there for a moment, as though trying to find the right words to say. She gestured to my futon for me to sit. I had no desire to have this talk with my sister, but I knew she'd just follow after me if I opted to leave and make this a public conversation, so I sat down.

"You tell people you've always been a playboy—"

"Because I have," I clarified.

Jackie shook her head. "No, you haven't. Sure, when you were in college, maybe, but that's what all guys do at that age." She bit her lip and chewed on it for a moment. "After Mom and Dad died, though, you changed."

"Yeah, well, death can do that to you." My jaw tensed up. I was on the defensive.

"It can. That's my point. When they passed away, that's when your heart hardened."

"Oh, please," I muttered.

"You may not see it, but I do, Finn. When you finally emerged from your mourning, you stopped caring. The girls you went out with after that never made it to a second date like they had before. Women became disposable to you. It was revolting to see you act like that, but I knew what you were doing."

Oh, this was rich. She really thought she had me pegged.

"I was trying to get laid," I said simply.

"No. You were hiding." Her voice was quiet. "Forbidding yourself to fall in love."

I felt the sting of her words and could no longer look her in the eye. I was afraid of what she might see, so I walked over to the window, keeping my back on my sister. "Yeah, well, what good is loving someone if they just up and die on you?" I watched people as they milled about Main Street, oblivious to the scene playing out above them. I spun around, leaning against the sill. "Look at Sam. She fell in love and look what's happening to her. Her heart is being ripped out and trampled on, and for what? Because she was a fool and fell in love." I shook my head again, vehemently this time. "No. Love isn't worth it."

Jackie came up to me then and hugged me.

"But it is, you big oaf. It is. Yes, it's scary as shit to risk getting hurt, but the payoff is in the joy it brings you. Don't be afraid to fall in love, Finn. It's the best feeling in the world. It makes the heartbreak worth it. I promise."

I shrugged out of her embrace. I knew what she was trying to do, and it wasn't going to work. I needed to forget Sam. Force her out of my mind. My eyes flicked over to the quarter bottle of Jack left on my kitchen counter. I went over and poured myself a shot.

"It doesn't matter." I downed the drink and poured another. "Go home, Jackie. Or go back to the hospital. Be with Maggie and Joe. Be the friend to him that I can't be." Instead of pouring another shot I drank straight from the bottle. "I'll leave tomorrow. Right now all I want to do is forget." If Jackie was going to be pigheaded and block me from making my escape today, then at least I was going to check out mentally.

With the bottle in hand, I headed for the darkness of my bedroom to drink the day and the pain away.

 Chapter 18

Jackie must have left at some point because I heard the door slam behind her. Good. I didn't need her to coddle me. I just wanted her to leave and let me live my life. I took another swig from the bottle and closed my eyes, waiting for the hurt to be numbed.

I must have passed out because when I awoke, it was to sounds in my kitchen.

A quick look at the clock and its glowing red lights indicated it was 6:27. I didn't know if it was a.m. or p.m., though.

My head throbbed, but I was alert enough to know there shouldn't be sounds in my kitchen. I reached under the bed for a bat I kept there. Being as careful as I could, I got out of bed and tiptoed to the door.

That's when I smelled coffee.

Someone broke into my house and made coffee?

Curious, I rested the bat on my shoulder and went into the kitchen and frowned.

"Jackie, what the hell are you doing?" I dropped the bat next to the door. She was cleaning up my dishes while eggs and bacon fried in the pans next to her. "I almost beat you over the head."

She looked up from the dish she was drying. She had no trace of a smile. "Careful. That's what I'm about to do."

"Beat me over the head?" I smirked. "Go for it. It can't be any worse than this headache." I walked into my tiny kitchen and sat down at the two-top table and looked down at the shiny surface.

"Hey, I haven't seen the top of this table in years," I marveled.

Jackie scoffed as she poured me a cup of coffee. "I wouldn't doubt it. You really need to hire a maid or learn how to clean up. This place is a biohazard."

She put the cup down next to me and went back to flipping the eggs.

"No offense, Jackie, but don't you have your own family to be playing mother hen to? Or is this your way of apologizing to me?"

Jackie whipped around, the greasy spatula pointed at me. "Apologize?" Her face got red. She let out a slow and controlled breath, the sort of thing she did when she was trying to count to ten before she blew her top. The spatula lowered, and she turned back to the pan.

I watched and waited for her real reason for being here as she plated some bacon and eggs for me.

"Mmm, breakfast," I murmured.

"It's dinner, jackass." Wow. My sister rarely cursed, which meant she was pissed. So was I. I didn't need her to mother me.

"All right. Why are you here? And what's with making me eggs?"

She sat down at the table and crossed her hands together.

"You need greasy food and caffeine for hangovers," she said as though that explained everything. "Plus, it was the only thing that looked unspoiled in your fridge."

That was probably true. Though I was a decent cook outside of baking, I ate out a lot. Making a meal for one was pathetic.

"Now, eat," she said, leaning back in her chair. It was clear she wasn't going to say anything more until I had.

Blowing out a frustrated breath, I picked up my fork and shoveled in the eggs in two bites.

"Okay," I said between chews, "I have food in me. Now can you tell me what the hell is going on? Why are you here instead of with your own family?"

She waved her hand. "You are my family, in case you forgot. And my family is fine without me. Nick's mom is visiting this weekend."

"Ah." There was the truth. "So you're hiding?"

The face she made indicated she very much was. I didn't blame her. His mother was a pain in the ass. Like mother like son.

"I told Nick I was at the hospital checking on Joe."

Joe. Ugh. I felt like an ass. I still hadn't gone to see him. What was worse, I'd thought so little about Joe these last few days.

"How is he?" I asked, though I wasn't sure I deserved the update.

Jackie shrugged her shoulders. "Okay, I guess. I mean, he's not okay. He just had a stroke, but they are gonna keep him there to monitor him. If he remains stable, they'll release him into some physical therapies, but even if that happens, it's gonna be a long road to recovery."

"I need to go see him," I said, nibbling on a strip of bacon.

"You do, but not today. Today you need to do something else."

"Yup." I nodded. "Leave town."

Jackie's hands clenched as she brought them in front of her, as though to steady her frustration, which was aimed directly at me.

"I understand your desire to run, Finn, I really do. And if that's what you want to do, I won't stop you. But before you go, you have to do one thing first."

I put down my bacon and leaned back in my chair. "I do, do I? And what's that?"

"You have to talk to Sam."

I shook my head, amused at the suggestion. "Um, no. I'm not doing that."

"Oh, you do, especially after I—" She stopped short and her eyes widened. She'd let something slip.

"After you what? Jackie, what did you do?"

She stood up and walked into the living room. I followed after. "Okay, so don't get mad, but after our chat yesterday, I *may* have driven over to the hospice."

My skin ran cold. "Ben, is he—"

"No, he's still kicking."

My heart slowed back down, but then I cocked my head to the side. "So why did you go there?"

Jackie let out a breath. "I had to know, okay? I had to know if Sam felt anything for you or not."

"Jesus, Jackie!"

"I know, I know! This is none of my business, but I had to know for sure if the woman who was breaking my brother's heart and forcing him to run away was someone he had to just get over, or if she was someone he had to fight for."

I laughed, amazed by her ignorance about the situation.

"You don't get it, do you? She loves her husband," I said as forcefully as I could, trying to make her understand.

She lowered her eyes. "Yes, she does."

The affirmation hurt more than it should have.

"But," Jackie continued. "I think she's also falling for you."

"Jackie," I said as calm as I could. "What did you say to her?" This was just like her to meddle into something she had no business being in.

"Nothing. I swear. It's what she told me."

Despite my best efforts to remain hardened, I felt myself daring to hope.

"Explain."

"Well, for starters, when she saw me there, she didn't say 'Hello' or 'What are you doing here?' You know, the normal response for someone showing up at your dying husband's bed after only meeting them once."

I waited for how that mattered.

Jackie came over to me and looked into my eyes.

"She didn't care about me at all, Finn. She asked where *you* were."

That's it? That's her basis for Sam falling for me? I actually laughed out loud. "So what?"

"She said she's been trying to reach you, but your phone isn't on. I told her you were dodging my calls." Jackie frowned at me, then reached into her pocket and handed me a handful of "While you were out" messages that I used at the coffee shop. "Tina saw me pull up earlier and gave these to me."

I looked down at the messages. Each one about an hour or so apart.

"So she left a few messages. Big deal." I didn't know what the fuss was about.

"Nine times, Finn. She tried to reach you nine times in one day. You don't message someone that many times if you aren't into them."

I looked at the messages written in Tina's handwriting:

That chick Sam called. Call her cell. I noted the number scribbled down at the bottom.

Sam called again. I told her you weren't here, but she checked in anyway. Call the chick.

OMG. She won't stop calling, dude. Like every hour now. This woman is batshit crazy. Maybe you shouldn't call her.

I looked up at Jackie. I supposed it was odd she called so much. I found my phone and turned it back on. There were five missed calls from her. "And you're sure her husband is okay?" I asked, staring at the number.

"He was still alive when I was there an hour ago. She said there had been no change."

The messages felt heavy in my hand.

"I should call her. Something's wrong."

"No, you should go see her," Jackie urged. "Finn, I'm telling you, there's something there. Whether she knows it or not or if she feels too guilty to believe it, she likes you. She's seeking out your company. You need to go to her because, damn it, you need her, too."

She was grasping at straws like I had been. I knew better, though. "You're wrong. She wants a friend."

"So what if she does? Are you seriously going to leave her at a time like this? What kind of friend would that make you?"

I frowned at her, but she was right.

"Go take a shower. Shave. Put on some nice clothes. But when you go, look into her eyes and see the truth that's written there."

I smirked. "Which is what?"

Jackie grabbed me by the arms and shook me. "That she's racked with guilt about having feelings for another man while the husband she loves is dying."

"Jackie, I know you think—"

"Just because she loves her husband, Finn, doesn't mean she can't also love you. Even her own husband can see that. Why can't you?"

I stood there frozen, hating myself for wanting to believe her.

"Finn, I'm right about this. You know it too. Deep in your gut you know she cares about you."

I blinked at her in response.

"Shower. Change. Go," she repeated.

I felt myself nodding. If there was a sliver of a chance that Jackie was right, I needed to know before I left town. And if she was wrong, then the road out of town would be an effortless one to take.

Chapter 19

I sat in the parking lot of the hospice for several minutes, trying to decide if I was ready to have my heart broken or not. What if Jackie had read the signs wrong? What if those messages Sam left meant nothing? What if she just didn't want to be alone?

My eyes caught my reflection in the rearview mirror. "Then you make sure she isn't alone, you selfish ass."

Rolling my shoulders, I adjusted my glasses and went inside to find Sam. The romantic in me envisioned marching inside, taking Sam by the hand, and pulling her into my arms. I wouldn't ask permission; I'd just grab the back of her neck and kiss her like I'd never kissed another woman before. Nurses would turn and look, at first shocked, but then they'd swoon at the romantic gesture. Sam would pull back, shaky on her feet, with a look of wonder that such a love was possible…

"Mr. Allen?"

I came back to reality and found myself at the front desk.

"Oh, sorry," I said, "I was lost in thought."

The nurse smiled. "It looked like a good thought."

I blushed. "It was, actually."

"Mrs. Whitman asked me to send you down to her husband's room if you showed."

"Oh. Right. Thanks."

She gestured down the hall, and I made my way toward Ben's room. My footsteps were quick and driven. The door to his room was open, so I poked my head in. I was about to say "hello" when I stopped short at what I saw.

Sam was in a fit of tears as she sat next to Ben, who appeared much weaker than I'd ever seen him. This was a bad time. "I can come back."

"No, come in, please," Ben answered.

Sam turned away from her husband, her hands covering her face. She looked utterly defeated. It pained me to see her so distraught.

"Perfect timing, Finn," he said, bringing my attention over to him. Ben patted the edge of the bed, indicating for me to sit.

"Ben, this doesn't concern him. You're tired. We can talk about this later. When you're more up to it."

Ben gave a weak little laugh. "Oh, my dear, optimistic darling." He looked over at her. "There aren't going to be any more good days. No, what few I have left are going to be riddled with pain. Soon, I will likely be too drugged to do much more than sleep." He reached out his hand to take his wife's. "You know this. You've spoken to the doctors. You know this is the only time."

More tears came, but she didn't protest any further.

"Now, Finn, have you given any more thought to my question?"

At that, I looked over at Sam, who was staring at me.

"I..."

"Ben...I—love *you*." Her voice was soft.

"I know that, peanut," Ben said, matching her tone. "But I think you might be capable of loving him, too." He looked up at his wife, not in an accusatory way, but in a way that granted her the permission.

"How can you ask me to marry someone else? We could have months yet..." I couldn't help but notice she hadn't flat out refused his request.

"Oh, Sam. You and I both know it's only days now. The time for waiting to see what might blossom between the two of you is over. What you feel for Finn may not be love quite yet, but there's something there. A spark."

She pulled away. "A spark? No. There's no spark. He's my boss. A friend. Nothing more."

Ouch. *Told ya, Jackie.*

"I may be old and I may be dying," Ben said, "but I'm not blind. And I can see the way Finn looks at you." Ben looked at me. My eyes grew wide as I realized I was looking at Sam. "Even now, he can't take his eyes off you."

"No! That's not what I do," I protested, standing up to give me some distance from my accuser, but I found myself losing steam. He was right. That was exactly what I did. No matter where I was, I sought her out, hoping to catch a glimpse of her. "All right, fine. Maybe I do, but that's only because your wife is beautiful." My face flushed as I felt Sam's eyes on me.

"See?" Ben said as though that settled everything.

Sam didn't look convinced. She crossed her arms defensively. "So because Finn thinks I'm...beautiful," Sam said, struggling to get the word out, "you think I should marry him? I'm not some prized mare that needs to be sold off!"

A cough ripped through Ben which made him turn red. Sam instantly got him some water and helped him sit up more.

"I'm fine, I'm fine," he chided. "And no, that's not the only reason I think you should marry him." He locked his eyes onto his wife. "And of course you don't need me to find you a replacement. It's only that…you're attracted to him, as well."

My breath caught as I waited for her reply.

Her eyes drifted to me for a fraction of a second before she sat next to her husband on the bed.

"Attraction isn't the same thing as love, Ben. You know that."

My heart began to beat faster. *Did she just admit she was attracted to me too?*

"It's what brought us together," Ben murmured. His eyes were kind as he looked at his wife.

She swallowed. "Ben, I'm not attracted to Finn."

And there it was—the knife to the gut. Though I knew it was the only real outcome, it still hurt like hell to hear her confirm it.

"Oh, poppycock!" Ben shouted, pulling my eyes back to them.

"I'm not!" she fired back.

"Prove it then."

She made a face. "Prove it? How am I supposed to do that?"

Ben's face remained calm as he considered her question. "I suppose you could kiss him," he said after a moment. "Right now, in front of me. That might prove to me there's no spark between you two."

I held up my hands in protest, but Sam stood up, her face determined.

"Fine," she spat. "If this is what it takes to get it through your thick skull that I have no interest in Finn."

Standing up, she pointed her finger at the space in front of her. "Get over here."

I blinked several times, trying to figure out if she was joking or if she seriously thought I'd kiss another man's wife while he watched.

When I didn't move from my spot she marched over to me. I held up my hands in shock, but she pushed right past them, not giving me a chance to restrain her. She grabbed me by the face hard and then planted the briefest and most chaste peck on my lips. It lasted a grand total of one second.

She pulled away and turned back to her husband, as though that settled the matter.

Ben frowned, and I knew exactly what he was thinking.

"You call that a kiss?" I challenged.

She hadn't put any effort into it. She barely made contact with my lips, and yet, even so, they longed for more.

She loved her husband. That much I knew. She and I wouldn't end up together. I knew that too. Ben's plan was ludicrous. I'd never agree to it, nor would she. But I also knew this would likely be the only time I would ever be granted the permission to kiss her as passionately as I dreamed of doing since the first day I met her. I wasn't about to let that opportunity go to waste.

Ben nodded at me when the look in my eyes made my intentions clear.

"*This* is a kiss," I whispered low and hot against her ear. I spun her around to face me and grabbed her wrists, locking her in place. Her eyes were wide from shock so I released her hands. I was relieved when she didn't slap me or push me away. Instead she looked up at me, almost daring me to do it.

That was all the encouragement I needed. I ran my hands gently up her body until her face was cradled securely in my hands. Her eyes closed in anticipation, and her breath hitched. I took one final look at her. My eyes were hungry as they lingered on that lush bottom lip that had been tormenting me from day one. I couldn't believe I was finally going to taste it.

Unable to wait any longer, my lips crashed into hers as though drawn together by a supernatural force. Her lips were soft and full, like a warm blanket welcoming me home.

At first, she tried to resist me. Her hands struggled in my hold, and her body was rigid against mine. I wouldn't force myself on her, but I just needed one more second, then I could let her go. Let the idea of her go. One moment longer and I could live off the high for the rest of my days.

My fingers released her hands, and I braced myself for her retreat, but it didn't come. Instead of pushing me away, her hands slid upward onto my chest and wrapped themselves tight in my shirt, pulling me closer. When her tongue brushed against mine, I nearly lost it. She was responding to me. She was kissing me back just as fiercely as I was kissing her I slipped my hands behind her back, pressing her body harder against mine, feeling her breasts firm against my chest. It wasn't close enough. No matter how much I felt her body on mine, it wasn't enough. I wanted more of her. And by the urgency of her lips on mine, she felt the same.

It was only when Ben cleared his throat that we tore our lips apart. Each of us panting a bit, a mix of shock and longing lingering on our faces.

"I think I've proven my point," Ben said.

I couldn't tell from his tone if he was pleased by the show or disappointed.

Sam wiped at her mouth, not looking at either of us. "Um, could you give us a moment, Finn?"

"Right, yeah. Of course."

Bewildered and completely confused, I left Sam to work out the aftermath of the epic kiss we'd just shared. A kiss that told me Ben and Jackie had been right. There *was* something going on between us. We desired each other, that much was clear. But was it merely lust or something more?

 Chapter 20

Once I left the room, I had to sit down. I had to process what had just happened. Sam and I kissed. In front of her husband, and she'd kissed me back. Of that I had no doubt. Her touch still lingered on my skin. The memory of her fingers when they dug into the back of my neck, the gentle, yet impassioned way she clung onto me...I hadn't imagined that. My shirt still held the wrinkles of where she'd grabbed it, pulling me closer. And her lips, my God, her lips. I'd never kissed a woman with lips like that. It was as though her lips had been molded to fit over mine. There was no awkwardness about it. No banging of teeth or a tongue that was too aggressive. It was as though we were in sync on a cosmic level. Our lips moved in time as though we were dancing.

Dancing.

The salsa classes... To think this whole ride began with my idiotic suggestion to take her dancing. I shook my head.

Now was not the time for me to try to stake my claim on Sam. Her heart was already spoken for. It likely would be for some time. What I could do, though, was be the kind of friend she deserved. From our conversations, I knew friendship was something she was lacking in her life. She worked and cared for her husband and thought little of her own needs. She had been the provider for countless months. Hell, she was even forgetting to eat. That was going to change as of right now. As her friend, I could help tend to some of her basic needs. I couldn't leave her. No matter how hard it might be for me to stay, I wouldn't abandon her.

"I need to go shopping," I said to no one in particular.

For the next hour and a half I traveled to just about every store in Bucksville. Naturally, the Shop and Go didn't have everything I needed. I could have made due with something else, but I had a specific plan in mind, and I wanted to see it through to the end.

When I returned, I carried with me a large wicker picnic basket in one hand and a soft throw pillow in the other.

Sam was lying down on a row of chairs out in the hall, so, at first, I thought she was asleep, but her head popped up when I approached. Against my will, my heart skipped a beat when her lips curled into a small smile.

"You came back." Her voice was still hoarse from crying.

"Of course. I had to run an errand," I said, placing the basket down on the floor.

"I'm sorry for the waterworks." Sam sat up and rubbed her thin fingers across her face as though to wake herself up.

"Not at all. You're allowed to break down. In fact, it's expected at a hospice. I would think you were a heartless bitch if you didn't shed at least a few tears." That garnered another small smile. "How's he doing?"

"He's sleeping. Again." She gestured to the open door. "I shouldn't have worked him up so much." She let out a long breath. "I know he's only trying to look out for me, but arranging someone to take his place…" Her hands rose up in an exasperated manner.

"I know. I had the same reaction at first." I sat down beside her.

"At first? Do you mean to tell me you agree with him now?" I could tell she wanted to scream at me, but she didn't raise her voice because she didn't want to wake Ben.

"No. Not so much agreeing…it's just…I guess, from a man's perspective, I can see where he's coming from."

That garnered a look of surprise. I laughed quietly at her expression.

"Wait, hear me out," I said, trying to defend my honor. "After my folks died, I got pretty overprotective with my sister, Jackie. She was going through a rough pregnancy at the time, and I watched over her like a hawk. I wouldn't let her go to the store alone. I held on to her elbow whenever I could." I shook my head. "Her husband actually had to step in and tell me to back off and let him take over that responsibility."

I closed my eyes in embarrassment, remembering that discussion almost came to blows. "I guess what I'm trying to say, badly, I might add, is that men are natural protectors. When someone we love is put in danger…we sort of go out of our minds trying to ensure they are safe. Rational thought doesn't factor in sometimes." I scratched at the back of my neck, trying to come up with better words to say. "It doesn't mean he loves you any less, Sam. In fact, I'd say it means he covets you. Can you really fault the man for trying to make sure his most beloved treasure is provided for?"

Sam looked up at me with her big chocolate eyes. I could see she wanted to believe what I was saying so desperately, but she was conflicted by the truth of it.

"I won't lie, Sam. I'd do the same if I were in his shoes."

I reached out then and took her hand and gave it a gentle squeeze. It wasn't a romantic or sexual gesture. It was an act of human compassion at a time she needed it. "I'm not going anywhere, Sam. I'm gonna be here for you. In any way you need."

She looked up at me, seemingly confused by my words.

"If what you need is a bottle of Jack and a shoulder to cry on again, I'm your guy." I reached for the basket and pulled out a mini bottle of Jack Daniel's and placed it beside her.

Her eyes lit up as she laughed but then covered the sound with her hand so as not to disturb her sleeping husband.

I reached back into the basket. "If you need someone to scream at about how unfair the world is, I'm your guy." I wagged a bag of earplugs in front of her, which earned me a smirk. Not to be deterred, I kept going. "If you need someone to go to the store and buy you all your favorite foods because you're too depressed or too puffy-eyed from crying to be seen in public, I'm your guy." I started pulling out an assortment of junk food and laid it all beside her. "I didn't know what you liked, so I went for a mix of salty and sweet and hoped I got a few of them."

Her face turned into one that was hiding back genuine emotion. She touched a can of Pringles gently and teared up.

"These are great, thank you."

"Oh, and I got you a pillow too, 'cause I know the ones here aren't so great." Placing the pillow on her lap, she latched onto my hand.

"Thank you," she whispered.

I shrugged but didn't release her hand. "Don't thank me yet. It's a bribe." I winked.

She cocked her head to the side.

"I'm still holding out hope for a salsa partner," I said, wiggling my eyebrows.

At that, she let out a sound that started as a laugh but quickly dissolved into a cry.

"Well, whatever your intent was, thank you."

"I'm here for ya," I said, knowing now I could never leave town. Leave her.

She wiped away a tear but smiled. "That's good to know, because I might need that shoulder to cry on now."

I pulled her to my chest and took her in my arms where she seemed to collapse. Her strength had been depleted. She couldn't be strong anymore. I held her tighter, trying to convey with just my arms that I wouldn't let her go. When that didn't seem to work, I found my voice.

"Anything you need, Sam. I'll be here for you." I held myself back from kissing the top of her head. "I promise. You won't have to go through this alone."

That's when alarms started to go off all around us. Sam picked her head up off my shoulder as a shout came from one of the nurses down the hall.

"Dr. Andrews! We need you in Room 12, STAT!"

Before I could blink, several things happened at once. Shouting coming from all directions. The squeak of shoes against linoleum. A rush of wind as people in scrubs whisked by us, and Sam, sitting up, ramrod straight. Her expression was unreadable.

Two words were allowed into my consciousness amongst all the chaos. "He's coding."

That's where things slowed down.

I looked at Ben's room then back at Sam. I expected to see her rush in after the nurses to become a permanent fixture at her husband's side, but she didn't. She remained seated.

Her eyes were on the floor. Her demeanor was calm. I started to wonder if she was going to pass out.

"Sam? Do you need me to help you up?"

She looked toward the room but gave no indication of what was going on in her head.

Without blinking, she whispered, "He has a DNR order."

I was no doctor, but I'd watched enough TV to know what that meant: Do Not Resuscitate.

"If he's coding," she said, calmly standing up. "They won't be able to help him." She closed her eyes. "And neither will I."

"Oh, God, Sam. I'm so sorry. I didn't know."

She stared down at her hand and twirled her wedding ring amid the sound of the beeping monitors a few feet away from us.

She looked up at me. "He heard us."

"Who?" I asked, taking a step toward her.

"Ben. He heard us talking. Or rather, he heard you."

Sam began to wobble a bit, so I grabbed her by the arm and held her upright.

"He heard you tell me you'd be here for me. That's all he needed." She shook her head a little bit again. "That's what he's been holding out for." Tears began to fall down her face.

A long sound of a single note from Ben's heart monitor echoed into the hall.

That was the moment when Sam finally let go of what little strength she had left and fell into my arms.

Chapter 21

It didn't take long to get confirmation of what we both already knew the second Ben's heart monitor sounded.

"Mrs. Whitman. I'm so sorry." The doctor came out with his hands clasped neatly in front of him.

Sam's head lifted up off my shoulder where I held her upright. I pressed my hand against her back for support, ready to catch her if she went limp again, but she surprised me by stepping away from me on her own two feet.

"Can I see him?" Her voice was surprisingly steady.

"Of course," the doctor said, gesturing to the room.

Sam took a brief breath, straightened her shoulders, and went in. The doctor and I stared at each other for a moment until he finally left me, giving me a gentle pat on the shoulder.

For a moment, I just stood looking at the door, waiting for the wailing from Sam to begin, but it never did.

Part of me wanted to leave her alone, but the stronger part of me needed to be there when she got out of that room. I promised her I'd be there for her, and I wasn't about to break that vow on day one.

When Sam came out, a good half hour later, she didn't say anything. She didn't even acknowledge that I was still there. Not that she could have seen me at all judging by how red her eyes were. She walked out of her husband's room and down the hall to the outside garden. I followed, keeping a short distance.

Once outside, she sat on the bench and looked out over the yard. I didn't say anything but walked over, taking up the spot beside her. I placed my arm on her shoulder to let her know I was there. Sam's face was vacant as she peered out into the night sky.

"One of the nurses told me when we first checked Ben in, to not feel guilty about leaving his side to go for coffee or to take a night off." She glanced down at her hands again, taking her wedding ring on and off as she spoke. "I assumed she meant I didn't need to worry about his medical needs, but she explained to me that, in her experience, some of her patients seemed to hold on, not because they wanted to live but because they knew their loved ones didn't want to let them go." She swallowed back her emotion as she struggled to get the words out. "She told me they would wait...until they were alone to pass on. They didn't want their family to have to endure the agony of watching them slip away."

She looked at me then but only for a moment. "That's why I was out in the hallway when you came. I could tell he was pretending to be asleep. I knew, without a shadow of a doubt, he was waiting for me to leave. He was waiting for his moment to die." She swatted away the tears that slid down her face, as though angry with herself for crying.

"So I got up, kissed him goodbye, and gave him what he wanted." Her eyes clouded over, and her bottom lip trembled as she tried to hold herself together.

At that, she turned to me again.

"What am I supposed to do now?" The question was so simple and so filled with fear that it broke my heart because I didn't have an answer.

Instead, I did the only thing I could do and pulled her into my arms and held her.

I don't know how much time we stood there, her fingers curled tightly onto my T-shirt, but when the outside lights came on, she seemed to register she'd been holding me for too long and abruptly let go, choosing to hold on to herself instead.

"Come on," I said when her breathing returned to normal. "I'll take you home."

She let out a semi-hysterical laugh. "What home? I don't have a home."

I nodded. I'm sure that's exactly what it felt like to her. Without her husband, their home would feel empty.

"I can't imagine how hard it will be to go back, but I can go with you. I'll stay as long as you want me to."

She shook her head and walked away, turning her back to me…shutting me out. The way she held her shoulders, I could tell she was already thinking about whatever things needed tending to before she could leave.

"Sam, we can deal with everything else tomorrow. For now, you go home and rest."

She surprised me by spinning around. "I told you, damn it. I don't *have* a home!" She brushed past me then and made her way back inside. Her pace was quick, determined, like she was trying to ditch me.

I followed after her, not sure what I had said to upset her so much, and found her back at the basket, downing the nip bottle of Jack. I approached her as one might a wounded animal.

"Sam, what's going on?"

She dug into the basket, looking for another bottle, but when she didn't find any, she grabbed a chocolate bar instead. She tore into it and took a bite. I waited impatiently as she chewed.

"What I mean, Finn, is that I don't have a place to hang my hat." She shook her head. "Ben hated hats, swore that's what caused balding." She looked up at my thinning hair.

"I was never a hat guy. This is just nature's way of tormenting me," I confessed, still not sure what she was talking about.

She took another bite and then tossed the unfinished bar in the basket before she continued with her explanation. "We got evicted from our apartment last month." She leaned back in the chair, her head resting against the wall. "The medical bills were just so much… I know I could have not paid them, but then Ben would have been mortified. He's a very proud man. *Was* a proud man." Her lip jumped again. "Was. I have to think of him in the past tense now, don't I?"

I could tell this was a dark road she was heading down, so I did my best to divert it for as long as I could.

"So, you two moved into something cheaper?"

She laughed. A deep and uncontrollable laugh.

"Oh, if only. We sold our house once in New York to combat the bills that mounted and moved to a small rental in Bucksville. Stubborn fool wanted to be close to the trees and away from the city while he got treatments. The sale of the house only gave us about ten grand after we paid back the bank what we owed on it… That held us for a while. Until we got behind on the rent. Once he moved into the hospital, I moved into our car." She let out a breath and rubbed her face "That got impounded a few days ago." She shook her head. "He never had any idea we lost the rental. He would have dragged himself out of the hospital bed, wires and all, if he knew I was homeless."

"Wait. Are you serious? You don't have a bed to sleep in?"

She sat up but didn't look at me.

"It doesn't matter anymore."

I looked at her with new eyes. She had been not only dealing with a dying husband, working three jobs, but was also homeless, too?

"He's left me with nothing. Not even him. Bastard." Her voice quivered along with her lip.

"Right. Well, then you're going to crash at my place until we figure something else out."

She waved me away. "I'm fine here. They won't kick me out. At least not tonight." She gave me a limp smile. "I am a grieving widow, after all."

She folded herself into one of the chairs and closed her eyes, dismissing me.

"Fine," I said. "Then I'm staying with you." I plopped myself into the chair beside her. "It's too bad you don't wanna come back. I have more Jack Daniel's at my place…"

She scoffed and opened one eye. "The last time I drank at your house, things didn't end so well."

I flinched. "Right. That was a mistake. Admittedly."

She closed her eyes and tried to ignore me again.

"Look, you need a place to stay. I have the room. You can rest, cry, drink, throw shit, whatever you want. And I promise I'll behave." Her eyes opened and she sat up, so I crossed myself for good measure.

"Finn, as wonderful as the idea of crawling into an actual bed and pulling the covers over my head for eternity sounds, I can't. I have to deal with this." She gestured to her husband's room. "There are papers I have to fill out, things I need to do…"

I placed my hand on her shoulders. "There's nothing that can't wait until tomorrow. I'll tell them we're leaving. I'll give them my cell if anything urgent comes up."

She looked toward the nurse's station then back at me.

"I'll bring you back here first thing in the morning."

"I can't ask you to do that for me," she whispered.

"You aren't asking me. I'm offering. No. I'm demanding."

She let out a deep breath, still unsure.

"Sam, I told you. You don't have to do this alone."

"Don't I, though? Ben's gone…"

I pulled her into an embrace. "I know he is. I can't change that for you. I would if I could, but I *can* help." I placed my hand on her face to tilt her toward me so I could look her in the eyes. "Let someone take care of *you* for a change."

She sucked in her bottom lip for a moment while she contemplated.

"Okay," she whispered once to herself and then once to me.

"Okay," I echoed, taking hold of her elbow to bring her home.

 Chapter 22

I'm not sure what I expected. Crying. Screaming. Anger. Those were all of the emotions I'd prepared myself for once we got back to my place and the mask she had to wear at the hospital could slip off. But she did none of that. I actually would have preferred it if she had.

Instead, I got nothing. From the moment she sat down in my car, I saw her entire demeanor shift. Her eyes focused on something unseen, and her body was limp. It was as though she had fallen asleep sitting up. I suppose that was to be expected. She was tired. She had to be.

For the next week, however, that's all she seemed to do: sleep. She locked herself in my room and slept the day away.

"What do you mean she just sleeps all day?" Jackie asked when she popped in for a surprise visit one day.

"I'm not sure if she's sleeping, necessarily." I shrugged, shooing her away from the bedroom door. If she was resting,

I didn't want to wake her. And if she wasn't, I didn't want Sam to hear us talking about her.

"She never comes out?" Jackie said, as I dragged her out of earshot.

I shook my head, glancing over at the door, willing Sam to emerge and prove me wrong. "I bring her in meals three times a day. Sometimes she eats, sometimes she doesn't. We don't speak. Well, *she* doesn't speak to me. I feel like I'm talking enough for the both of us, though."

Jackie frowned. "She needs to talk to someone, Finn. Maybe you should call a doctor or something."

I waved a dismissive hand at her. "No. She doesn't want to talk. She will. When she's ready."

"Finn…"

"Was I any different after Mom and Dad died?"

Jackie started to object but had to bite her tongue.

"No. I wasn't. There was nothing anyone could say to me during that time, just like there isn't anything to be said with Sam. She needs time to mourn in her own way."

"But the funeral—"

"Is being dealt with," I assured her.

Ben had actually left pretty specific instructions in his will. He didn't want any formal service. Not even a celebration of life. He simply wanted to be cremated then buried in the earth with a young sapling so that his energy could feed the tree. He had clearly had some time to think about his final resting place. "I've made all the arrangements. The tree is on hold at the nursery, and his ashes remain at the ready, whenever she is."

Jackie started to speak, but I held up a finger.

"And not a second before."

She seemed annoyed but didn't push the subject.

"I actually don't think we'll get to put the sapling in until spring anyway. It's getting too cold. But that might be for the best. She might be stronger in the spring."

"There's something else I wanted to talk to you about, Finn."

I nodded, anticipating what was coming. I hadn't been to work since taking Sam home. I'd sort of shoved the shop onto Jackie, and while I knew she could handle being the boss, it wasn't fair to leave her in the lurch.

"I'm going to start working again tomorrow. I promise."

She gave me a small smile.

"And what about Sam's shifts?" There was a tone in her voice that indicated she was annoyed with Sam's grieving time.

My nostrils flared. "I'll take them on, too."

Her hand reached up to rub my shoulders. "Then who will be here to make sure Sam's okay? You can't be in a hundred places at once."

"I won't let you fire her," I said with an expression that told her I wouldn't back down on this. She had no idea the hell Sam had lived through. I wasn't about to let her lose her job too.

"She's not going to lose her job, bonehead. But I do think we need to hire Tina on permanently. At least until the baby's born. She needs a paycheck and she's changed, Finn. You haven't seen it. She's on time, she's taking orders correctly, and is actually nice to the customers."

I raised an eyebrow at that.

"Hand to God." Jackie laughed. "I couldn't believe it either. Something has changed in her. She has a purpose now. A reason to want to do a good job."

Sighing, I scratched at the back of my head. "That's not really my call. The shop is yours. You can hire anyone you want. Hell, if you need to fire someone, fire me. I can live off the inheritance for a while."

Jackie's eyes rolled back into her head the way they did when she was exasperated by my idiocy.

"I'm not letting anyone go, you oaf."

I gave her a hug then flopped down on the couch, exhausted from the whirlwind of the last few days.

"What you're doing for Sam is noble. It's the right thing to do, Finn. Don't ever question that. I just worry about my brother. I wonder sometimes who is looking out for him, you know?"

"I'll be fine." I glanced at the closed bedroom door. "Just as soon as she is."

The next few weeks passed in a sea of silence as Sam continued in her retreat inward. It was to be expected. She had suffered a devastating blow. She was drained, mentally and physically.

While she healed, I opted to work the morning shifts as that seemed to be when Sam was the least active. It was a bitch to wake up so early after staying up late every night on the off chance she emerged and wanted to talk. I needed to be ready for her, whenever that day came.

My normal routines began to change in those weeks, too. Instead of drinking a few beers and binge watching TV until all hours, I found myself not wanting to sit still. Dishes were washed after they were used. Bags of trash were taken to the curb the second they were full. Hell, the mop was even run over the floor on a weekly bases instead of a yearly one. I polished up my guitar, too, though I hadn't bothered to tune it yet. I didn't want to disturb her. So I cleaned. Quietly. The apartment needed to have order when she came out. She had enough chaos in her life. I didn't want where she was staying to be one of them. It was stupid, but it gave me a purpose. Something I could do with my time while I waited for her to come back to reality.

As it was, there was little I could do to console her, save bringing in her meals and taking care of her laundry. She wore my clothes these days, and let me tell you, she rocked my T-shirts way better than I ever did. I chatted my head off when I visited, if only to hear myself talk. I wanted her to have a sense of normal, so I talked about the most trivial things: shows I'd watched, what I was planning for dinner, where I put the lilac soap she seemed to like.

While I was getting ready for bed, my cell went off. I frowned when I saw it was my sister.

"What's wrong?" I asked. Jackie never called unless there was something important. She knew I didn't like the phone to ring. I didn't want to risk waking Sam.

"I wanted to let you know I finally tracked down the lot where Sam's car was towed. I paid the fine like you asked. I had it towed to the back lot. The keys are in my office if you need them. There was a suitcase in the trunk. It didn't look like there was anything valuable, just some clothes, so I left that in there. Want me to bring it up?"

I signed in relief. "No. It's fine for now. I'll grab it later. Thanks, Jackie."

"How's she doing?"

I knew she was getting sick of asking that same question. The answer was always the same: "no change."

"Honestly, I think she's getting better," I said.

"Oh?"

Walking over to the bedroom, I pressed my ear to the door and heard the soft sounds of her snoring. "Yeah. She's eating more. She actually looks at me now when I walk into the room, and she seems to be showering more often."

"All good signs," Jackie confirmed.

"I think so. I wish there was something more I could do for her, though. I feel so useless."

Jackie sighed. "Finn, you're doing more than most would do. You've been an angel to her."

I wasn't sure about that, but I let the comment slide.

"Hey, do you know where I can buy guitar picks? I can't find any in my case and my nails aren't long enough these days." I was eager to start playing, at least during the hours I knew Sam would be up.

"I think Josh has some. Let me look." The phone rustled while she went to her son's room.

"Does he ever play the one I got him last year?"

More ruffling sounds. "God, he's a pig," she huffed. "Um, he did after the lessons you gave him, but he needs more help if you ever stop being a handmaiden."

I smirked. "You know you'd do the same for me."

"I *did* do the same for you, or have you forgotten the pathetic waste of space you were after Mom and Dad died?"

I ignored Jackie's jab. She didn't nurse me back to health so much as she nagged me out of bed to the point of wanting to kick the crap out of her.

"Finn, I can't find anything in this sty he calls a room. You might wanna try Bert's," Jackie said. "He always has the most random things in his shop."

It was true. Bert's Bazaar Tackle & Gift Shop did have just about everything. But his inventory fluctuated depending on whatever crap he got in from his vendors. His place wasn't the best for reliability on a product, but if anyone in town sold guitar picks it would likely be him. I could have driven the forty minutes out of town to the nearest big-box store, but I wasn't about to leave her alone in her condition for so long.

I jotted down a note for her, like I always did when I left, on the off chance she came out while I was away. If I went fast, I'd be home within the hour and could have dinner in the oven before Sam woke. I still needed to get some mozzarella for the lasagna and a loaf of garlic bread. There was ice cream in the freezer for dessert already.

Opening one of the cabinets in my kitchen, I noticed I had plenty of basil left. I smiled at the neatly organized spices. I'd turned into quite the cook these last few weeks with Sam here. I loved that I had someone to cook for, a reason to break out the old pots and pans. Sam was quickly becoming the reason I did just about everything these days. A dangerous thing indeed.

I was consumed with dinner recipes running in my head, that I almost didn't hear the shower running when I got back. Glancing at the clock, I noticed she was up earlier than normal, so I busted butt to get dinner in the oven. She tended to be the most alert after her shower, and I wanted to be able to take advantage of that.

While the lasagna baked, I dug out the pink picks Bert had. They were clearly for a small child's guitar judging by the neon shade of pink, but they would work for now.

Ripping open the small bag with my teeth, I fished out a pick and sat on the futon to tune my guitar. I strummed quietly, twisting the keys to the right notes until I was satisfied, humming gently as I did.

"You play?"

My head whipped up. Sam was standing in the doorway of my bedroom. Her hair was wet, dripping haphazardly on one of my gray T-shirts. It was a V-neck and too big on her, so it hung off one shoulder in that delicious '80s *Flashdance* iconic way.

"You're awake," I said, moving the guitar over my lap to hide my body's inadvertent reaction to seeing her looking so undeniably sexy.

She nodded and walked into the room. "Don't stop on my account," she said, addressing the guitar.

"No. It's fine. I'd rather know how you're doing."

She looked down at the floor.

"Would you hate me if I blew your question off and just asked to hear you play instead?"

She sat down near me, tucking her leg under herself as she did. I watched her carefully, trying to figure out her mental state, but was coming up short.

"Please," she asked.

I flushed suddenly. I don't know why I was embarrassed. This was what I lived for back in college. "I'm kind of rusty," I confessed. "It's been a while since I played."

"You're stalling," Sam said.

God, it was good to hear her voice.

I laughed at her perceptiveness. "Yes. Yes, I'm stalling. Um…what do you want me to play?"

She shifted in her seat. "Do you know 'Longer' by Dan Fogelberg?"

"Sure." I couldn't believe she knew that song. "My mom loved that one. It's one of the first songs I ever learned."

She bit her lip as I began plucking out the chords. I had only made it through the first few lines before she started crying.

"Sam? What is it? What's wrong?"

She lifted her head, and I saw that her eyes were red.

"I'm sorry. That was our wedding song. I don't know why I asked you to play that." Without another word she pulled herself off the couch and went back to the safety of my room.

"Shit."

 Chapter 23

The oven buzzer went off about an hour later, and I debated whether or not I should bring her in a plate. I hated that I had forced her back into her shell. *Damn it. Why did I agree to play that song?*

I walked over to her door to listen. The sobbing seemed to have stopped. My hand rose to knock on the door, but I hesitated. She probably didn't want to be around anyone at the moment. Then again, she had to eat.

Determined, I marched into the kitchen and pulled the lasagna out of the oven. I grabbed her tray and put a plate in the center. I dug the lasagna out with the spatula, using more force than was needed for the task which resulted in spilling hot marinara sauce all over my T-shirt.

I cursed and looked down at the carnage that lived on my shirt. It was everywhere. I looked like I was in a slasher flick. "Seriously? What the hell is it with me and keeping shirts clean?"

The heat of the sauce was about to burn my skin, so I reached behind my back and yanked it off with a single tug. Beyond pissed, I tossed it to the floor and kicked it across the kitchen for good measure.

"Well, this day can kiss my ass," I grumbled as I finished plating Sam's dinner.

After preparing some small salads for us, I sliced up the garlic bread, being careful not to cut my damn thumb off. I set my serving at the table, where I'd learned to eat like a civilized human being these last few weeks, and put the rest on Sam's tray. Scooping her food up in one hand, I went back to her door and knocked.

"Hey, Sam…I don't know if you're hungry, but I've got dinner ready. Is it okay if I come in?"

I waited, not expecting to hear anything.

"Yeah. I'm okay," she said.

Opening the door a crack, I poked my head inside.

"So, you might wanna look away," I said to Sam, who looked up at me, confused. I felt my face redden. "I may have spilled sauce on my shirt and had to take it off…"

"You spilled something on yourself?" She giggled. "Again?"

Her laugh lured me inside, making me forget for a moment that I was half naked. Sam's eyes widened, but then she quickly looked away.

"Sorry," I said, rushing into the room to set the tray down. "I should have waited for you to avert your eyes. No one needs to see this body sober." I was seriously wishing I had the physique I'd had twenty years ago. One that wasn't quite so soft in the middle and was a hell of a lot tanner.

"No. It's fine," she said. Her eyes peeked up at me for a moment. "This is your house. You should be able to wear whatever you want."

"Oh, well, that's a relief because I usually walk around in the buff."

Her eyes flew back at me.

"I'm kidding."

"Oh," she said, a wicked grin on her face.

"Well, I'll grab a shirt and leave you to your dinner. I hope you like lasagna." I turned to go to my dresser when she stopped me.

"Have you eaten yet?" she asked.

"Um. No. Not yet. Mine's on the table. I always serve you first. Why?"

Her eyes softened. "I thought we could eat together?"

This time, it was my eyes that widened. "Of course. Sure. Whatever you want."

"Thanks. I'm starting to go a little stir-crazy looking at these ugly walls."

I smirked, despite the jab. They were pretty awful. Boring white, with dents and chips that needed mending. "We don't have to eat this crap if you don't want. We could go out somewhere if you want."

"Oh, no. I don't think I'm ready for that quite yet, but a table and chair would be a good start."

I nodded in understanding and went to get her tray. Her hand reached out and touched mine. "And your food isn't crap. It's actually quite delicious."

"Thanks." My face broke out into a goofy grin.

She pulled back the covers and followed me to the table.

"Hey, you cleaned," she said, looking around the apartment for a minute before joining me at the table and curling her bare foot under her as she sat at down.

"Yeah," I said. "It helped pass the time."

Sam poked at her food with her fork. "I'm sorry to have been a burden."

I laughed. "You haven't been. You've been a godsend, actually. I think if I hadn't cleaned when I did, the EPA would have come in here and taken me out in a biohazard container."

She laughed, but it was half-hearted.

I went over to the table and sat across from her. I took her other hand in mine until she looked at me.

"You're not a burden. I've enjoyed being able to look after you. It felt...good." And it did. It wasn't a line. I enjoyed taking care of Sam.

She glanced at me shyly then smiled. I gave her hand a final squeeze and let her go.

"This smells great," she said, gesturing to the lasagna.

"I hope it tastes good. I tried a new recipe." I stood up to grab the salt and pepper then realized, in horror, I still hadn't gotten a shirt on yet.

"I should probably put on a shirt, huh?" I laughed.

Sam snickered. "I don't know...maybe you should wait until after dinner. After all, you might get sauce on you again."

Nodding, I looked down at my sauce filled plate.

"Even so. It's a bit nippy in here." That earned me the laugh I was going after.

Once in my room, I leaned my head against the door and chided myself for being flirty with her. Sam wasn't mine. I had to remember that. Keeping my damn shirt on would be a good way to start.

Our conversation over dinner was casual. Light. I didn't bring up Ben and neither did she. I made no mention of how long she'd been shut away in the bedroom or on any topic that might stress her out. I didn't want to say or do anything that might set her off again.

"Thank you," she said after dinner was finished.

"Not a problem."

I got up and brought our dishes to the sink.

"Not about dinner," she said, following after me. "I mean, thank you for everything you've done for me." Her eyes were downcast as though she were ashamed of asking for help.

"Hey, there's no need to thank me. I told you that you could stay as long as you needed and I meant it."

She looked up at me. Her eyes were searching for something. Assurance maybe?

"This is a guilt-free zone, okay? It takes as long as it takes. No one grieves the same."

That garnered a small nod.

"Although," I admitted, "you and I have very similar ways of dealing with loss."

I turned the water on and began to wash the dishes. Without being prompted, Sam came to stand beside me, ready with a cloth to dry them.

"How old were you when your parents died?"

Though it had been ten years, it still hurt to think about them.

"I was in my mid-thirties. Old enough to know they weren't going to last forever, but to lose them so close to each other...it just seemed so—"

"Unfair?"

"Yeah," I admitted. "I was pretty useless back then. I was still living with my folks." I flinched at that gem. "Still working at the goddamned coffee shop and foolish enough to think there wasn't anything my guitar and a quick screw couldn't fix." I paused and looked down at the soap bubbles as they popped silently against my hands. "I was so lost. I knew I'd blown my chance to make something of myself. I was really floundering. Then they both died within months of each other, and I sort of went off the deep end." I passed her a plate. I could feel her eyes on me, urging me on. "I shut myself in my room for a good month." I glanced over at Sam. "I have you beat there. You only lasted sixteen days. Pathetic." She smirked then smacked me with the dish towel.

"What made you emerge from the darkness?"

I took in a deep breath. "My sister, Jackie. She wasn't as hip as I am about you needing your space. In fact, she didn't give a rat's ass about what I wanted. She would barge into my room. Jump up and down on my bed, rip open my curtains, anything to get a rise out of me." I shrugged. "One day the urge to rip her head off was stronger than my desire to stay under the covers."

Washing the last of the silverware, I rinsed them off and set them on the towel on the counter before Sam could dry them.

"My point, is that we all heal in different ways. So you don't need to thank me. I'm just glad you're talking again." I smiled. "It's nice to hear your voice. I've missed it."

She smiled. "Thanks. It's good to be heard." Her shoulder bumped me playfully. I couldn't help but smile. It was so good to have her back.

The rest of the night we watched mindless reality TV or wherever the clicker landed on. She didn't seem to care what was on the screen. Neither did I. The fact she was sitting in the same room with me instead of hiding from the real world was good enough for me.

At some point during the evening, she got up and went to bed, with a quick "Night" before she retreated back into her room.

I stared at her door for several minutes after she left, wondering if I'd see her again in the morning. Somehow, I knew I would. She wasn't back to normal yet, but she was back to functioning. Baby steps.

Although it was almost the end of October, we'd gone through a warm snap the last few days, making me curse myself for taking out the AC unit last week. The open windows provided little relief from the heat, and I was sweating in places that one shouldn't sweat. Too hot to care, I stripped down to the buff and kicked off everything but the sheet. If it hadn't been for Sam in the next room, that would have landed on the floor, too.

When I woke the next morning, it was to a cool breeze on my backside. It felt nice after sweating most of the night. I was about to drift back to sleep when I heard a slight chuckle.

At that, my eyes flew open. A quick assessment of my surroundings informed me that I was lying in bed, face down, spread eagle on the futon, sans sheet.

I froze for a moment as I realized the view Sam was getting in the full sun of the morning.

"Morning," she said, trying to hold in her laughter.

I reached my arm onto the floor, searching for the sheet, but it wasn't there.

"Looking for this?" Sam asked.

I turned my head as much as I could without rolling over and saw her standing there with the limp sheet in her hands.

"Um. Yes, please."

She bit her lower lip and tossed it to the bed, mercifully landing and covering my bare backside.

I pulled it around my waist and sat up.

"I guess you weren't lying earlier when you said you like to walk around naked," she said with a playful lilt.

I willed my face not to flush any brighter than it already was. "It was really hot last night," I said, holding the sheet around my lower half as I stood.

"It sure was."

The sound of her voice was husky. Almost longing. I shook my head. I was imagining things.

She stood in front of me, one hip jutted out to the side as her hand played aimlessly with her hair that was wild with sleep. She was still in my shirt from last night. Damn. That woman was breathtaking.

"You're up early," I said, trying to shift the focus away from my nakedness.

"So are you." She nodded toward the sheet.

I didn't need to look down to know what she was referring to. Mornings and hot women warranted a response.

Shifting my hold on the blanket to hide my erection, I brushed past Sam.

"I'll just be in the shower."

I hurried into the bedroom to the sound of her soft giggles. The fact that she was being playful about the situation confused the hell out of me. I knew she was making the best out of another awkward situation, but it sent my head some mixed signals. Was she as aroused as I was or was her laughter a result of nerves? Or, worse, was she making fun of me?

When I got out of the shower, I saw that Sam had left me a note on the bed.

Sorry I snuck a peek at your backside. Guess that makes us even for the whole dream-induced breast fondling thing.

A small winking face was scribbled beneath it.

I cocked my head to the side, more confused than before. Was she flirting? No. She'd just lost her husband. She was apologizing. That was all. *Don't read anything else into it.*

Throwing on some jeans and a T-shirt, I went out to the kitchen and found Sam at the stove flipping some scrambled eggs.

"I hope you're hungry," she said.

"Starving, actually." I walked into the kitchen and started setting the table.

She brought the frying pan over to the table and scooped out the eggs at the same time the toaster released its catch.

"Butter or jam?" she asked.

"Both."

She paused in the kitchen and smiled. "Me too."

While she put the pan back on the stove, I grabbed the knife and began spreading the toppings on her bread.

"I added some ham, cheese, and pepper into the egg. Hope that's okay?" She sat down across from me, looking nervous.

"It smells wonderful. Thank you." I gave her a genuine smile. "You didn't need to do this."

She reached out and took my hand for a moment.

"Yes, I did. I need to feel useful again."

I nodded, completely understanding.

After we'd had a few bites of breakfast in shared silence, she dropped her fork and looked up at me wide-eyed.

"Oh, shoot. I forgot to make your coffee," Sam said.

"Sit," I insisted. "I'm in the mood for tea anyway. I'll make you a cup, too." I pushed away from the table and walked over to my pantry and opened it. A healthy selection of teas was stacked neatly on an eye-level shelf. "I have, um, Earl Grey, Chai, Peppermint, Sleepy Time—no, probably not that one, Green, Breakfast Blend..."

"Wow. I didn't know you were a tea connoisseur."

"I'm not. I knew you didn't like coffee, so I stocked up on tea."

"Wait. You bought all of this for me?"

I turned around and was surprised to see Sam right beside me.

"I didn't know what kind you liked, so I asked Jackie to pick me up a variety each time she did a grocery run. I knew, one of these days, that bedroom door was going to open and you were going to need a cup of tea. I wanted to be sure I had your favorite."

Her eyes welled up as she turned to look at me. One of her hands cradled the side of my face.

"Thank you," she whispered.

I wanted to press my face farther into her hand but settled for the feeling of her skin against my morning stubble instead.

She withdrew her hand then as though thinking better of it and placed it instead on a box of tea. She lifted it off the shelf and sort of held it there for a moment.

"I have a confession to make," she said.

I looked down at her with expectant eyes.

"I hate tea."

"What?" I said, laughing.

She joined me in the amusement. "I know…it's just, Ben drank it and I was young when we met, and I wanted to impress him, so I told him I loved tea and, well, after that I was stuck in the lie."

I noticed her face didn't crumple when she said his name like it had last night. Instead, she was smiling. It was slight, but it was there.

"So let me get this straight," I said, trying to keep the mood light. "You don't like coffee *or* tea?" There was no hiding the horror in my tone.

She shrugged. "Since I'm spilling truths today, I guess I should also clarify and say that I've only ever had coffee once. Someone brought me a black coffee instead of my tea years ago at dinner." She shivered. "I almost puked."

"Well, that explains it then," I said, feeling relieved.

"What does?" It was Sam's turn to look confused.

"You haven't given coffee the old college try."

She started to protest, but I gestured to the collection of teas.

"How many varieties of tea have you tasted?"

She made a face of resignation. "A lot."

"Are there some that tasted worse than others?" I pressed.

"Well, sure," she said.

"So that stands to reason you may not have tried a coffee you like." I grabbed her shoulders gently with an excited glee.

"Sam, there are literally hundreds of ways to have coffee and black is one of the most vile and bitter ways to drink it."

She looked at me, doubtful.

I placed my hand on my chin to think. "I see you as a Caramel Macchiato type of girl."

Sam gave me the smallest of smirks. "You're just saying that because it's my favorite drink to make."

"See? It's fate then." I beamed down at her. "I know what we're doing today."

"We?"

I nodded. "We're gonna try some coffees."

"Finn," she hesitated. "It's not that I don't want to..."

"But?"

She looked down at the oversized T-shirt and sweats she was wearing.

"I don't exactly have any clothes here."

"You do, though!" I suddenly remembered her suitcase. Brushing past, I held up a hand. "Wait here."

I flew down the apartment steps and grabbed the keys to Sam's car from a very confused Jackie in the office. In less than five minutes I was back upstairs, with her suitcase in hand.

"Where did you get that?" She gasped.

"It was in your car. I had it towed to my lot in the back."

Sam stood there staring at the case, almost as though she was afraid to open it. After a few moments, however, she took a few tentative steps toward it and knelt down in front of it as one might kneel in front of an altar.

"I'll pay you back..." she said softly. Her eyes were intent on the suitcase.

"Don't worry about it," I said, but I could tell it landed on deaf ears.

She didn't say a word as her fingers worked the zipper, ever so slowly. She took a small breath before she threw back the cover, revealing two neatly packed sides of clothing. The left side held two pairs of shoes: a pair of black heels and a white pair of sneakers, and then four rolled up garments.

Sam unhooked the latch that caged the clothes in and grabbed one of the rolls. It looked like a pair of jeans.

She laid the roll on the ground and unraveled it, revealing, not only a pair of jeans but buried within the folds, a T-shirt, flannel shirt and socks, underwear and a white bra.

"Dude. How did you...?" I looked down at how she'd packed the entire outfit in amazement.

"When you live out of a suitcase, you learn to be efficient in packing."

"I'll say. That's amazing!" My eyes drifted back to the bra for a moment longer.

She didn't say anything as she placed delicate touches on her clothes.

"Is that your uniform for the coffee shop?" I asked, pointing to the tan roll.

"Yeah. The other one is what I wear at the mailroom, and this is what I clean Mr. Davenport's office in," she said, pointing at the roll closest to her.

"And what is that one?" I asked.

Her fingers touched the dark fabric. "This was supposed to be for his funeral."

I knelt down beside her, unsure of what to say.

"The jerk didn't even let me have that," she sniffed.

"I don't know. I think I sort of agree with him for not wanting a funeral," I admitted.

She looked over at me with teary eyes.

"I mean, no one wants to feel sad. Why invite a bunch of people over to bring everything back up again? I don't think I want a funeral either. Too depressing."

Her shoulders slumped.

"Don't be mad at him, Sam. I just don't think he wanted you to have to cry anymore."

"Too late," she said, picking up the black dress and unrolling it. "It was his favorite dress." She held it up, showing off the V cut at the neck, backless, and a skirt that flared. It was one hell of a sexy dress for such an occasion. I raised my eyebrows.

"I know. It's not really a funeral dress, but when paired with this very modest sweater it looks appropriate. No one would know what was underneath, except him. That seemed fitting somehow."

She rolled the dress back into the tight roll and placed it gingerly in the suitcase.

"Guess I'll never get to wear that again."

I pondered for a moment. "What if you could? We could have a funeral here. Right now. Just the two of us?"

She cocked her head to the side. "No. I have a better idea." Reaching over, she touched the dress and a cosmetics bag affectionately, and then stood up. "After an afternoon of binge watching several episodes of *Supernatural*, I know what we're going to do tonight."

"Okay. Whatever it is, I'm in." I realized in that moment, I would do anything she told me to. That probably wasn't a good thing.

 Chapter 24

Later that night as Sam put on her dress in the bathroom, I fumbled with my tie in the bedroom. I hated ties and hadn't worn this suit since my aunt's funeral last year. It was a bit snug in the waist, but it was the only nice thing I owned. If Sam was wearing a dress like that, I couldn't very well slap on some khakis and call it a day. I had to at least attempt to match her even if she was way out of my league.

There would be no leaving the damn apartment at all if I couldn't get the knot of this tie figured out. I cursed under my breath and then again when the bathroom door opened.

"Jesus," I whispered.

Sam stood in the doorway looking sexier than I'd ever seen her…well, except for when I saw her beside me in my bed. That was going to be a hard memory to pass but this night, this moment, was a close second. I couldn't help but let out a low whistle, which seemed to make her blush.

Her hair was elegantly pinned up on top of her head. A few strands came down in thick curly tendrils, tempting me to touch them. On her lips, she wore a rose color that made her eyes pop. It was the dress, however, that could have knocked me over with a feather. The neckline was much lower than it had appeared when she held it up, and the silky fabric hugged every luscious curve of her body. She seemed to float as she walked toward me, a smile on her face.

"Holy hell, that is some dress," was all I could say.

She laughed and began to help me with my tie.

"Now you see why Ben liked it."

I took another not so discreet look at it.

"Yes. Yes, I do."

She lowered her eyes, indicating I had embarrassed her, but seriously…how could one woman be so hot?

"Almost got it," she said, bringing my focus back to her hands as they worked the silk fabric. It was adorable how her face contorted as she worked. When she was satisfied, she patted the knot once.

"Thanks," I said, as she stepped away. "How did you learn to do that?"

She shrugged. "Ben liked to dress up for church. Toward the end, he didn't have a lot of strength, so I learned how to do it."

I walked over to the mirror to inspect her work.

"Very nice."

"I'm multi-talented."

I turned around and saw she had a hand stretched out.

"Come on. We don't want to be late."

My forehead wrinkled.

"Late? For what? Where are we going, Sam?"

She had a mischievous look in her eye. "You'll see."

And with that, I took her proffered hand.

She led me out of the apartment and down the stairs with an urgency I couldn't place. Her hand shook against mine as we walked. I wasn't sure if she was gathering the courage to keep holding it or if she was trying to break free of it. Either way, I wanted her to make the choice, so I held on as lightly as I could to make it easy for her, but she didn't let go.

"So, do you plan to tell me what's going on?" I tried again.

She was about a step ahead of me, half-dragging me down the sidewalk. People we passed were lifting an eyebrow at our odd behavior. I could only shrug back at them. I didn't know what was going on either.

"Are you abducting me?" I asked as we ventured farther down Main Street. "Because if you are, you don't need to pull so hard. I'll go anywhere with you willingly, you know?" As soon as I said that, I wondered if I should have. It revealed more about my thoughts than she probably wanted to hear. It was difficult to keep things platonic, however, when she was holding my hand and looking as fine as she did.

"There's a place I know Ben would have wanted to see me in this dress," Sam said over her shoulder, as though that settled the matter.

A few steps later, she stopped and turned to face me. Our hands were no longer touching.

Her posture straightened as though she was willing strength from deep within her.

"What's wrong?" I asked.

Her big brown eyes looked up at me.

"Nothing's wrong. We're here."

I cocked my head, wondering how the middle of the sidewalk was "'here.'"

Turning around, I saw we were in front of the drugstore...and the Salsa Studio.

My eyes widened.

"You're going to dance with me?"

Her bottom lip curled inward, hiding behind her teeth.

"Well, it *is* Sunday...so I thought, maybe we could try it. For Ben."

I nodded in understanding. This wasn't a romantic move. It wasn't a night for us. This was an obligation to her late husband. I was a fool to have gotten my hopes up.

"Right. Of course," I said, trying my best not to show my utter disappointment.

I'm not sure why it mattered to me that she only wanted to dance to honor her late husband's wishes when I was hoping for the same thing before he passed. Just a few weeks ago, I would have given anything to be granted permission to be that close to her. To have my hands on her. Now it seemed more like I was a consolation prize.

"Are you okay?" Her expression changed to one of concern. So much for my acting skills.

"Sure. Of course. Let's dance."

I wasn't very convincing.

"This wasn't a good idea. I'm sorry. I shouldn't have dragged you here—"

Grabbing her hand, I held her still.

"It's a great idea, Sam. Honest. I'm being a selfish jackass. Ignore me. I would be honored to dance with you."

Her face examined mine for a few moments as though pondering my answer.

"Why are you being selfish?"

"Look, just forget it, okay? Let's go in." I spun away from her peering eyes. My hand pulled hard on the door, but it didn't budge.

"Um…it's locked."

"Locked? Are they closed?" Sam's voice sounded confused.

I scanned the door for some indication until I found it. Near the door, under their normal business hours was a small handwritten sign: Closed for floor waxing. Open Monday at 2:00 p.m. for Mambo Mammas.

"Mambo Mammas?" Sam giggled.

"I got dressed up for nothing." I sighed, yanking at my tie. "Now what?"

She took my hand again. "Keep your shirt on. It's time for Plan B."

I let her lead me again, back down the sidewalk. There wasn't much open on a Sunday early evening. The few shops that were open would be closing within the hour. That was a downside to small town life. One of the many downsides. Normally, it didn't bother me. I had the local bar and a fast food chain if I got the munchies. I hadn't needed much else, but tonight I was really wishing my town had more to offer Sam and her sexy-as-hell backless dress.

She walked us through the rest of the block and down another, past the town's post office and all of the downtown area. The night sky was creeping past us as we walked farther down High Street. She gave no indication of where we were going.

She didn't stop walking until she reached our town's small cemetery. My feet slowed along with hers as she entered the park.

"Sam, you know Ben's not here, right? He's in a jar in my living room…waiting for you to plant him somewhere." I started to wonder if she remembered me showing her the urn at all. I knew she was out of it, but surely she would remember that, wouldn't she?

Sam gave me a small smile.

"I know that, silly. There's something about cemeteries. I love them. It's so quiet, you know? It's one of the only places I can go to think."

She let my hand go and walked farther into the cemetery. My feet stayed where they were, the baggage of feelings with cemeteries holding me in place.

"They don't bite, you know?" Sam teased.

Feeling foolish, I pushed my feet forward and joined her on a nearby bench. A streetlight on the main road flicked on, protecting us from any ghouls in the night.

"So this is what you wanted to show me?" I gestured to the headstones surrounding us.

"No. Not really. I just wanted a quiet place to talk with you, I guess."

"I see."

Sam looked up at me. "Is this place making you uncomfortable? We can leave if you want."

She stood up, but I tugged at her dress to sit her back down, yet she stood firm.

"I'm fine. Really. I'm only uncomfortable about whatever it is you're not telling me."

She smiled. "Am I that transparent?"

I shrugged as she sat back down beside me.

"No. I can just tell when you have something on your mind, that's all."

Sam nodded, looking down at her hands.

"Ben could always see right through me. I guess you can too."

"What's wrong, Sam?"

She swallowed and began playing with the hem of her skirt. "I have been trying to figure out a way to tell you something, but I haven't been able to find the words. I'm sort of hoping the cemetery will help clear my mind so I can communicate it to you."

I shifted to look at her. Her brow was crinkled with concern.

She took a slow, but deliberate, breath. "I've been thinking a lot in the last few weeks. Nothing but thinking, actually." Another breath, this time quicker. "Ben was the love of my life."

"I know that." It broke my heart to say it, but of that truth, I had no uncertainty.

"My mother abandoned me when I was eleven. I lived with my aunt who didn't have kids of her own and really didn't know what to do with me. I tried to help as much as I could around the house but read in my room as often as I could." Sam shook her head. "I read a lot of books but never romance. My aunt wouldn't let me read those, even when I was in high school. She thought they lied to women, convinced them that love was just a page a way. Which it wasn't, she lectured me.

"She was the sort to give it to me straight. She drilled into me how rare and precious love was." Sam tucked the loose curl around her ear. "A girl would be blessed if she was able to find love in her lifetime because most didn't, my aunt said. So, when Ben came along, I knew I'd hit the jackpot." Her eyes were glassed over, but in pride, not remorse. "I fought like a wild dog to make him mine.

"You see, he had serious reservations about our age difference. We loved each other, for sure, but it took a lot of...convincing"—she smirked—"before he came to terms with my age. He felt as though he'd be taking advantage of me, you see, but what I tried to tell him over and over again was that I was his from the first moment I laid eyes on him."

She wrapped her hands around her waist, no doubt imagining his hands against her. It broke my heart.

"Yeah," I mumbled under my breath. "I know the feeling."

Mercifully, Sam didn't hear my comment because she went on talking. "When Ben got sick, my heart began to harden. Like I could actually feel myself shutting down. I became quite bitter and pessimistic at the unfairness of it all. It was so hard for me to find joy in life. I couldn't relate to my friends anymore. They all had these normal lives with healthy spouses. They went on about their daily business as though my entire world wasn't falling apart.

"Eventually, they stopped calling, and I stopped reaching out. I only am in contact with my Aunt, but she's in Florida and can't help much. Since he got sick, my life became engrossed in sustaining his."

I nodded silently, appreciating her honesty. It couldn't be easy to talk about.

"I'd convinced myself that once he was gone, I would die alone. I'd resolved myself to that. It was easy to imagine because I'd been blessed with the love of my life. I wasn't foolish enough to think it would come knocking again."

I waited for her to continue, but she had her face buried in her hands. When she finally looked up, she was glaring at me.

"Finn, I had a plan." Her voice shook with a sudden anger. "I knew what I was going to do after my husband passed away. I was going to move out of town and start life over, away from the memories. I'd even picked out the names of the fifteen cats I would own."

"Fifteen?"

Sam nodded her head vigorously.

"Yep. They were going to be named after characters from *The Hobbit*, but now I can't do any of that."

"Why not?"

She really wasn't making any sense. Maybe she'd emerged too soon from her mourning.

She stood up and threw her hands over her head.

"Because you ruined the plan, Finn!"

I cocked my head to the side, thoroughly confused. "How exactly did I ruin your plan to become a crazy cat lady?"

She'd gotten quite angry by this point. "By throwing a wrench into the well-oiled machine of my mourning."

I turned to face her, trying to get her to look me in the eye. She was holding something back.

"Sam, I don't understand—"

She turned away from me, forcing her eyes off mine, which felt like a rejection. She shivered against a sudden breeze that made the leaves in the trees shake.

I removed my jacket and placed it over her shoulders, being careful not to touch her for long. She seemed to want her distance from me. I just didn't understand why.

"See? This. This right here! You being a gentleman and giving me your jacket. It's not helping, Finn!" She spun around to face me.

"What? I thought you might be cold."

She shoved her arms inside the sleeves and pulled it close to her. "I *am* cold. The fact that you noticed...the fact that you took me in when I had nowhere to go. The fact that you gave me a job when you didn't even like me. It's all too much." Her voice was climbing up octaves as she spoke, increasing the level of hysteria.

I placed my arms on her shoulders to try to calm her energy. It seemed to work because she took a few slow breaths before she spoke again.

"Sam, what is it? What's going on?"

She ran her hands across her face again; a pained expression lived beneath her fingertips.

"I know I'm supposed to be grieving the loss of my husband, and I am. I think the bags under my eyes prove that, but I'm also...conflicted." The last word came out slowly, carefully considered before spoken.

"Conflicted by what?" I asked.

Sam let out a slow, measured breath.

"I'm conflicted by all of the thoughts I have...about *you*." Her voice was small, as though she were afraid to say the words out loud.

It felt like my heart stopped. "What sort of thoughts?"

At that, Sam made the cutest of frowns.

"I think you know *exactly* what kind of thoughts."

I reached out and grabbed her hand, finding her eyes as I did.

"Sam, I don't want to make any assumptions where you're concerned. I've blundered things before, especially with you, so I need you to be crystal clear about what you're saying."

Her eyes found mine in that moment; a steely determination was set in them.

"I haven't been able to get you out of my head. Especially after I woke to your hands on my body. And then that kiss Ben made us have. Jesus! That kiss! I wasn't prepared for that. I didn't expect to like it, let alone be turned on by it. I mean, it stirred up emotions I thought I was never going to feel again for another person."

I began to enjoy where this line of thought was going. Encouraged, I took a step closer to her. Clearly, that was the wrong move because she put a hand on my chest and pushed herself away.

"But then I got to thinking. Maybe that kiss was a fluke. I hadn't been intimate with my husband for a while, so that kiss may have been my pent-up sexual frustration. I mean, it *had* been a while."

My ego deflated. "Ah. I see." I took a step farther away.

"Which is why I think we need to do it again," she whispered.

"Come again?" I asked, unsure if I heard her correctly.

"I think," Sam said, dragging out each word, "we should try kissing again."

"To see if there are still sparks?"

She nodded quickly. "Strictly for research purposes."

My brain was having a hard time computing what she'd just said. She wanted me to kiss her. Again. She was having some feelings about me. There was no time for hesitating. I knew what I had to do. Like magnets, my hands cupped her face and held her there, locking eyes with her to make sure this was what she wanted. She licked her lips in anticipation and took an intake of air, bracing for impact. I held her there, our lips close, but not yet touching.

"Are you sure?" I asked, trying to rein in my desire. I didn't want her to feel pressured into anything. "You don't have to do this. You don't have to prove anything to me."

Her eyes flicked up toward mine. "I'm not doing this for you. This is for me. I can't move on with my life until I know what you mean to me."

I pulled back a bit so I could see her face.

"You want to know if I'm a rebound or something more?"

Sam swallowed. "Sort of." Her breath was coming in quick succession, causing her chest to rise and fall. In that damn dress, it was distracting as hell.

I considered her proposition. If I kissed her now and there was nothing between us, any possible future I'd envisioned with us would be gone. On the other hand, there could be no future with Sam unless I was able to break down the walls around her heart. It was a lot of pressure to put on one kiss.

"Screw it," I said. "If this is the only chance I get to kiss you again, I'm taking it."

Her hands wrapped around my waist, pulling my body closer to hers.

"Then kiss me already," she whispered.

Chapter 25

With everything riding on this one kiss I had little time to consider how I wanted to approach it. On the one hand, I could go in slow and hope for passion to follow, or I could dive in and kiss her hard enough to express the urgency of my need to feel her lips on mine and pray her desires matched. Either approach had its potential for disaster.

As I gazed down at her, wondering how I was going to screw this up, her lips found mine instead. There was nothing slow about her kiss, just a raw and burning need. Like a woman dying of thirst finally drinking her fill. It was animalistic and frenzied. We each fed off the other's soft moans and wandering hands.

My body responded not only to her tongue as it slid next to mine, but also to the firm grasp she had at the nape of my neck. She was pulling our mouths together, forcing the kiss to continue. Not that I had any plans on stopping it.

When her other hand latched onto my left butt cheek, however, I nearly lost it. Our bodies were pressed close enough that there could be no denying my erection against her. She didn't move away from it, but rather shifted her hips to be closer to my length, which made it very, very hard to think.

This was dangerous territory for us. Kissing…in public. In a cemetery, no less. Not the ideal spot for a make-out session.

With great difficulty, I pushed away from her, breaking our connection. We couldn't do this. Not here. Not now.

"I'm sorry, but if I don't stop now we might get arrested for indecent exposure," I panted.

The way she bit her bottom lip indicated she was thinking something very similar, which made the retreat from her more painful.

She reached up to unpin her hair, which had fallen loose during our experiment. It fell over her shoulders in lush waves, making my fingers ache to return to it.

"Well, so much for our connection being a fluke," she said nervously.

With my body now back under my control, I took a step forward and reached for her hand. She accepted it without hesitation.

"Damn it," she said, looking down at our hands. "Damn Ben for being right."

She leaned her forehead against my chest. My lips found the top of her head instinctively.

"Well, to be fair, he was a smart man."

"Very. He had a PhD."

Her hands wrapped behind my back as we held each other in a gentle embrace. I held on to her for a moment longer before I laid my cards on the table.

"Sam, I think it's abundantly clear now that I've had feelings for you since the moment you stepped into my office." I swear she stopped breathing for a second.

"Granted, they were hostile feelings at first," I continued, "but as I got to know you and the type of woman you are...I found myself in an unfamiliar place."

She lifted her head up to meet my gaze, encouraging me to continue. "When I first met you in college, women held no real importance to me. Their company was only required in the short term. Women were disposable to me, Sam." I flinched at my own confession. "But ever since I saw you again, I can't get you out of my head, and it scares the shit out of me. You were married. I couldn't fall in love with a married woman! That was just wrong on so many levels. Of course, that proved to be something of a unique situation in its own right."

She nodded. "I'll say."

"The point I'm trying to make is that just because your husband has passed away, I'm not going to pounce on you. I know you have stuff you need to work through, emotional baggage you need to unpack. The last thing I want to be is a rebound relationship. Not with you."

Here came the hard part of this conversation. I released Sam from my grasp to run my hands through my hair. It was a poor substitute for her body.

"We can't jump head first into this. Whatever this is. We have no idea what we're dealing with here. So I say we go slow. You can continue to crash at my place for as long as you need. If you feel up to coming back to work, Jackie said your job is waiting."

"And you and I?" she asked. Tears welled in her eyes.

"Sam, please don't think of this as a rejection. It's killing me to not drag you back to my apartment and have my way with you right now."

Her hands wrapped around her waist. "It is? Then I don't understand."

She didn't get it. I couldn't be a throwaway relationship for her. She had to be crystal clear with what she wanted because my heart was on the line. I honestly didn't think I'd be able to bounce back if she ended up discarding me.

"Your husband just died, Sam." Her chin began to tremble, so I held it in my hand. "I refuse to let you be a fling. *If* you and I ever get together, it's going to be for the long haul, and I need you to be ready for the same ride. I don't want us to go down two different paths from the start. It's too important. I want you to have the time to know what it is that you want. I don't wanna screw this up."

She looked at me for a long time, as though trying to process everything I'd said.

"So we just hang out. As friends?"

I nodded. "For now."

She mulled that over. "So what do friends, who also live together, do, exactly, when they find themselves all dressed up and nowhere to go?"

"Well, I wouldn't say nowhere." I glanced back at the town, which had darkened to twilight in our graveyard conversation. "Although there's not going to be much open at this hour."

Sam smirked at me. "I know just the place. I hear they make killer Caramel Macchiatos."

I laughed out loud at her suggestion.

"Finn, I appreciate your hesitation here. It comes from an honest place." The way she looked at me confirmed that she believed what she was saying. "But there's something you should know about me."

"Yeah? What's that?"

"I fight for things I want."

My pulse began to quicken at the implication.

"And I know what I want," she said with a small grin.

She gave her hair a flip and looked up at me with a seductive look that could only mean she meant me. Then she turned back toward the coffee shop.

"Well, hot damn," I whispered, allowing myself a window of hope as I ran to catch up with her.

When we got to the coffee shop, I insisted I make her coffee. I wanted my creation to be her first. Tina looked at me funny when I jumped over the counter to make it, but I didn't care.

It took exactly *one* sip of a Caramel Macchiato before I knew I'd converted Sam to the dark side. The way her eyes rolled back in her head and her sigh made the point abundantly clear.

"Damn," she said, whipping the foam from off her upper lip. "Why didn't you tell me about this sooner?"

I took a sip of my espresso and smirked. "I tried. Several times. You didn't believe me."

"No, I did not."

I was grinning like a schoolboy, but I couldn't help it. Sam was sitting across from me drinking coffee. I could hardly believe it was real.

"Hey, are you sure you're okay with this?" I asked.

"What? You breaking my coffee virginity?"

"No, um, this whole friend thing," I replied.

She hadn't exactly said "yes" to my offer. But she hadn't said "no" either. Still, she was here. With me. That had to mean something.

"I think you were right. My head is in a pretty screwed-up place. Jumping right into bed with you, while sure to be fun, might not be wise."

She reached across the table and squeezed my hand.

"Thank you. I don't want you to ever be confused about what it is you want and why you want it. You don't owe me anything. I need you to know that." I locked eyes with her. "Just because I've fallen ass over teakettle for you, doesn't mean you need to reciprocate. Understood?"

She grinned at me in a flirtatious way.

"And if I did?"

"Then we'd take it slow," I said. "I've rushed things with women my entire life, Sam. I'm not going to screw this up with you. I'm just not."

My resolve was firm. Though it was torture to resist the way she looked at me. Jumping into bed with a woman was the old me. It was time to try the slow and steady approach. Even if it killed me.

 Chapter 26

It's been a year since Sam and I began our unofficial dating. Neither of us openly called it that, but we'd slowly evolved from friendly conversations to long walks, lingering dinners and movies curled up together on the sofa. Yes, I finally broke down and bought a real couch which I slept on until properly invited into the bed with Sam.

There was a gentle transition into something "more," but neither of us had put any sort of label on it. We'd done nothing more than hold hands, as two close friends might be inclined to do. Well, and maybe cuddle on the couch.

It started out merely as offering her my protection during a scary movie. I playfully asked her if she wanted me to hold her through a gruesome scene, and she eagerly tucked herself under my arm. My chin rested naturally on her head, and thus began our fallback position whenever we watched a movie. Scary or not. We watched a lot of movies those first few months.

It was only when we started moving in time with each other that we finally got our groove on. On the dance floor, that was. Salsa Sundays had become my favorite day of the week. Not only because I got to put my hands on her and pull her close but because in those thirty-minute sessions, I was the one in control. I got to dictate where her body went. It wasn't the power trip I loved, but the trust she'd placed in me to lead her down the right path. She was counting on me to be her guide. There was something very primal and chest-pounding about that feeling. In those moments, I felt like she was mine, and I was hers. We'd claimed each other on the dance floor.

"What are you thinking about over there?" Sam asked, tossing a water bottle at me.

I caught it and grinned before I took a long drink.

"Our dance."

The smirk on her face told me she didn't believe me. She knew I wasn't a good liar around her, and I loved that she knew that about me.

"Okay, fine. Us then."

Our session was over, which meant I had to control where my hands went now.

She came over to me as other couples were changing back into their street shoes. I picked up our bag when I saw the owner, Ms. CeCe, chatting with the couple waiting for their private lesson once we cleared out. She was talking with a couple in their late thirties early forties, I guessed. They were both heavyset and neither of them appeared to know the first thing about dancing, judging by the wide eyes on their faces.

The woman looked more nervous, although the guy looked greener than normal. I smiled. They reminded me of when Sam and I first started coming to class. We were both so nervous around each other, afraid to get close but longing for it just the same. Learning to dance with someone was a whole new level of intimacy. I wished them luck.

Sam tugged at the bag, pulling my focus back to her.

"What about us?" Her hair was slick with sweat, and her face was still pink from exertion. How she could look so irresistible while sweaty and gross was amazing.

"I was thinking about how awkward we were when we first started class."

Sam made a face in remembrance. "We were awful."

"Beyond awful," I agreed. "We were so insecure with our bodies and each other. So self-conscious about how others might perceive us."

Sam nodded as she hooked her arm through my elbow and guided us out of the studio.

"Not to mention there were several people who raised a few eyebrows at our pairing." She laughed.

I couldn't argue with her. It was true. The locals were less than kind at first. Sam and I had several strikes against us. Mine all had to do with my oversexed past, while Sam was an outsider seemingly trying to find a new husband. They didn't know the truth.

They weren't with us from page one of our story. All they got to see were juicy middle bits. I suppose it would be impossible to feel compassionate about a relationship you didn't see from the beginning. Still, it didn't give them the right to judge us.

"Is that what we are? A pair?" I asked, taking Sam's hand, a habit we couldn't seem to break. If we were in a room together, our hands sought the other's out.

We walked down the street swinging our hands gently, our jackets buttoned tight around us against the nip of the winter air.

"A pair?" Sam repeated as though rolling the word around in her mind to see how it felt.

"Yeah. You and me. I know we don't talk about what we are to one another but, I dunno, is it time we tried to figure it out?" A new layer of sweat crept across my brow. I'd deliberately not brought up the subject because I didn't want to scare her away. Or worse, have her confirm my biggest fear: that we were having fun but that she didn't see a future with us. That was usually my line to a chick. *It's not you, baby. It's me. I'm just not ready to settle down yet.* The roles were reversed, and I didn't know how to handle it.

Her face grew somber, which I took to be a very bad sign.

"I suppose it's time for this discussion, isn't it?" Her voice sounded off. She was acting timid, and Sam was never timid. Something was wrong.

We walked down Main Street as my world froze in the balance. Was this where our time together ended? Had I somehow crossed a line? One look at her downcast eyes, and I had a sinking feeling my bubble was about to be burst.

"Look, we don't have to talk about it, if you don't want to," I said, trying to buy a few more days, weeks, or months of happiness before she swept it out from under me.

She stopped walking. Her hand slipped out of mine and retreated into the depths of her winter jacket. The simple gesture felt like a punch to the gut. She was pulling away from me already, and I didn't know why.

"No. I think you're right, Finn. It's time to talk. There are things I need to get off my chest before I burst."

The air drained out of my lungs. She was at a breaking point in our relationship. That's why she'd been so quiet these last few weeks. She'd been avoiding eye contact lately...having hushed conversations with Jackie and Tina. I'd assumed they were talking about birthday gifts for me, but in reality, she'd been planning her exit strategy. My mouth went dry.

I couldn't look at her. My eyes focused on the toe of her boot and the sound of the snow crunching beneath it as she fidgeted. "Is this the kind of talk we need to have in a crowded public place, or can we go back up to the apartment and have this talk over a drink?"

"A drink might be a good idea for both of us."

I risked a glance up at her, hoping against hope that maybe I'd misread the situation, but the way her eyes were still glued to the ground confirmed my fears. She couldn't even look at me.

Unbelievable. My nostrils flared, suddenly angry that this was happening. Hadn't I done everything for this woman? Hadn't I turned my life upside down just to make her happy, and now she was just going to walk out on me? I hated how chauvinistic that sounded in my head, but I clearly wasn't thinking logically.

"Right," I said. My voice was hollow.

We walked the half a block back to the apartment in silence. My stomach was flip-flopping between rage and heartbreak. I felt on edge, like I wanted to punch through a wall or at the very least, shout at the injustice of it all at the top of my lungs.

I forced my way up the stairs, flexing my hands into fists, with each step trying to release some of my anger. Once inside the apartment, I made a beeline to the Jack Daniel's and took a swig right from the bottle.

"Whoa, save some for me," Sam said, taking the bottle out of my hands.

She took a longer drag than I had.

Jesus. This was gonna hurt.

She handed it back to me then walked toward the window. Her shoulders were tense. I considered putting her out of her misery. I could tell her not to bother with her sob story and just go. I'd pick up the pieces, somehow. But I couldn't. I was too angry to let her off the hook. I felt blindsided, and she was going to give me a damn explanation, even if it killed me in the process.

Swallowing down the lump in my throat, I ground my teeth together. I needed her to say it to my face. I had to know why things didn't work out. I had to know what I'd done wrong.

The whiskey ran down my chin as I took another swig from the bottle. Nothing mattered more than dulling the blow. I pointed the bottle in her direction.

"I know what you're about to say."

Sam took in a breath as her eyes grew wide. "You do?"

Shaking my head, I looked at the ground. "Yeah, it doesn't take a genius to figure it out."

She blinked a few times in apparent disbelief.

I looked past her, out the window. I couldn't seem to look her in the eye at the moment. I didn't want this memory of her to be the one that forever lodged in my mind.

"How do you know what I'm going to say?" she asked.

"Remember. I know you better than you know yourself." I hated how pained my voice sounded. I could actually feel pieces of my soul splinter apart.

"That's true." This time her voice sounded small. "Still, this can't really come as a shock, right? I mean, this is always where we were headed. I think we've both always known that."

I knew it. I was a rebound.

"Just get it over with, would ya?" My fists clenched a few times as I tried to keep my disappointment in check. I knew I was acting like a dickhead, but I couldn't believe this was actually happening. I couldn't believe this was where our story was ending.

Sam's eyes narrowed, seemingly perturbed by my reaction. Did she honestly think I was going to make this easy on her?

"Finn, what is it that you think I'm going to say?"

I brushed past her and flopped down onto the couch and kicked my feet up onto the coffee table. It was a habit I'd given up while Sam was living here, but now that it was ending it seemed appropriate to reclaim my bachelor pad.

"This is going to be your 'Dear John' letter."

"My what?"

"You know? A 'Dear John' letter? Where you let me down easy and explain that 'It's not me, it's you,' or some horseshit, right?"

"Finn—"

"Oh, Jesus, Sam, just spit it out!" I stood up and stormed over to her. "You're breaking up with me, I get that, but what I don't understand is why. What did I do? I thought things were going well. Slow, yes, but I thought you were happy. You never told me otherwise. So how was I supposed to know? I'm not a mind reader, you know?" I grabbed onto her arms with more force than I meant to and gave her an urgent shake. "You have to tell me why I thought what we had together—this thing I felt in my bones...in my goddamn bones, is now gone."

I let her go when I saw that she was crying. I took several steps away from her, ashamed of myself. I'd behaved like an animal, but I was so lost and hurt. "I just need to know why,

Sam. Then you'll never have to see me again. Please," I begged. A sudden weariness fell over me. I'd accepted my fate and was now searching for the meaning of it all.

She sank down to her knees and sobbed.

"You want to know what you did?" she asked, with her eyes planted on her shaking hands. "You made me feel loved. Cared about. Hell, you made me believe I could be happy again." Her voice was cracking through her anger.

"And you're mad at me for that?" I asked, confused.

"No, you moron. I'm not mad at you for that."

"Okay then, so why are you breaking up with me?" I asked, exasperated beyond belief.

She took a few slow breaths, a gesture she reserved for my most idiotic behaviors.

When she looked up at me she had repositioned herself on one knee. A small silver band sat in the middle of her outstretched hand.

"I'm not breaking up with you, Finn. I'm asking you to marry me."

Chapter 27

"Wait...what?" I asked, staring down at the ring in her hand. My heart began thrumming in a wild and erratic pattern as my brain tried to process what I'd heard. Clearly, I had misunderstood.

"Finn, I swear...you're one of the kindest, most decent, and most hardworking men I've ever known, but sometimes you're an idiot."

I grabbed her elbow and helped her stand up. "I agree with you about your last point, so could you please put me out of my misery and tell me what the hell is going on?"

Sam took my hand and guided me onto the couch to sit me down. I was watching her every facial expression, looking for some indication that I'd misheard her.

"You and I... We've been going at a snail's pace," Sam began.

My forehead crinkled, offended. "A snail's pace?"

Sam frowned at me. "You haven't made a single move on me."

I looked down at our interlaced hands.

"Holding hands doesn't count," she whispered.

Had she wanted me to make a move and I hadn't seen it? The last thing I'd wanted to do was muck that up by making unwelcome advances, but had I misread her? Had she been giving me signals and I'd turned a blind eye to them?

"I was trying to give you space," I confessed, wondering if I'd somehow screwed this whole thing up.

She looked up at me with a small smile on her lips.

"Couldn't you tell I didn't want it?"

I stared at her dumbfounded. I'd been a fool. I'd ignored all signs my gut was telling me out of sheer determination not to alienate her by doing something wrong, but in the process of protecting our friendship, I may have missed out on having something more with her. Had I made her feel undesired? That was a question I needed to rectify immediately.

"Sam, it's not because I haven't wanted to make a move, believe me. I have, it's just..." I was fumbling for some sort of excuse that wouldn't sound as pathetic as the truth. I was scared I'd lose her. Sam held her hand up to stop my attempt to formulate my thoughts.

"I've been thinking a lot about this, and either you wanted to see if we could work as a couple before you made your move *or* you've been deliberately keeping your distance so you can cut and run."

The fear on her face as she said that last sentence was palpable and it broke my heart. Clearly, I hadn't done my job in assuring her of where my motivations lay.

"Sam." I squeezed her hand. "I'm not going anywhere. You're right about keeping my distance, but that wasn't for my benefit. It was for yours."

She cocked her head, not understanding.

"I was allowing *you* the space to leave if you wanted."

She nodded as though confirming her suspicions. "That's exactly why I decided to propose to you, since you didn't seem to be taking the hint."

My mouth opened and then closed. "Hint? What hint?"

She leaned over to me, so close that her breath was hot against the stubble of my cheek as she spoke. "I've tried everything, Finn. My lips against yours in the cemetery that night failed to convey my desires. My hips in your hands as we danced these last few months have struck out, too." She leaned back and licked her lips. I swallowed. "Even my eyes mentally undressing you every day hasn't done it…"

"You mentally undress me?" I asked, pushing up my glasses.

She smirked. "Every. Single. Day."

This was new information. I mean, I knew how I felt about Sam, but I never assumed she reciprocated the same feelings for me. I mean, sure, we were friendly and comfortable with each other, but I didn't think she was on the same desire scale as I was. Still…that wasn't a reason to propose marriage. Not that I wouldn't marry her in a heartbeat, but this seemed a bit irrational.

"You know, you don't have to put a ring on my finger in order to get me in bed," I said, wiggling my eyebrows to break the intensity of the moment.

"I didn't take you for the old-fashioned type," she said, smiling.

I reached out and took the ring from her hand and held it up to her.

"You don't have to promise me forever, Sam. I'm not going anywhere. If this is what you want, a more serious and intimate relationship with me," I said, blushing, "then I'm all in. I don't need a ring to tie me to you."

"But what if *I* do?"

Her eyes glistened over with an emotion I didn't understand.

"Sam, what is this about?"

She stood up and began to pace the small expanse of my living room. Her shoulders were tense, and her bottom lip tucked firmly under her front teeth as she thought.

"The first time Ben got sick, we were in New York watching a show. We had to leave before the curtain went up." She paused to wipe away a rogue tear before she continued. "He went from having an upset stomach to not being able to walk without pain in a matter of hours." Her eyes had fully glassed over by now. I knew it was hard for her to speak about Ben, so I didn't interrupt. "He was so weak by the time we got to the ER, Finn. He passed out. They rushed him into one of the rooms and put him on some heavy painkillers that put him to sleep, so I wasn't allowed to see him."

"Why not?"

"Because I didn't have his name at the time. I was a modern and independent woman and kept my maiden name, so they didn't believe we were married. My ring was at the shop because I'd needed it cleaned, naturally, so they didn't believe we were husband and wife. Mistress, maybe." Her voice began to shake as she grew angrier. "I had no proof that we were actually married. Nothing in my wallet had his name on it. He didn't have a Health Care Directive…" She wiped away more tears with the back of her hand. "I actually had to drive home in the pouring rain in the dead of night and dig through our legal papers to find a copy of our marriage certificate before they would grant me access to my own husband." She took a few deep breaths. "You can bet I changed my name to his after that visit. My point being, that I am in complete agreement with you about marriage being meaningless when two people love each other. It's a piece of paper, nothing more. Except when that piece of paper matters." She sat down next to me. "If something ever happened…I don't want to be denied access to you."

That was an answer I hadn't prepared myself for.

She pulled her emotions back in check with a quick breath. "Not to mention that you may not be old-school, but I am. I didn't even stay overnight in the same house as Ben until we were married, so living here in sin with you is kind of a big deal for me."

"Really?" That surprised me for some reason. "So you never banged Ben before your wedding night?"

My comment lifted the tension and she laughed.

"Oh, no, we had sex. Lots of it, in fact. I refused to move in with him, though. Sharing someone's living space...that's way more intimate to me than sex. When you move in with someone, you're not only sharing their bed but their life."

That's exactly what Sam and I had been doing. We were "roommates." We were sharing our lives together. We woke up at the same time. Ate most of our meals together. Picked out movies and took walks after dinner through our now beloved cemetery. Without realizing it, she'd become the reason I woke up in the morning with a smile on my face.

"So you're saying you want me for more than just my body?" I asked, smirking. "You want all this too?" I gestured to my tiny apartment.

"Well, we'd have to get a better place than this. No offense. In fact, a rental opened up on the hill. You know that big yellow house with the big oak tree in front? It's only a one-bed, one-bath, but it's way bigger than this place, and I don't know…it feels like fate somehow. Like it's a house we're supposed to live in."

"You've already been looking at places for us to live?"

She bit her lip again. "No, not actively. I saw a sign up at the Shop and Go. It looked perfect for us…"

I gazed at her in awe. She'd spent some serious time thinking about this. Her proposal wasn't a spur-of-the-moment decision. She was already planning our future together.

"I mean, if we moved, I'd probably need to find a better paying job…" she continued.

"Wait. You'd leave the coffee shop?" Somehow I assumed she'd never want to leave working alongside me.

"Finn." Her voice was kind. "I have a BA I haven't done anything with. I was a stay-at-home wife for years with Ben. Then I was a workaholic once he got sick. I'd love to find a job that will actually use my degree. Something meaningful and useful."

I nodded in understanding. "I know what you mean. I have a degree in music that I don't use either. It's frustrating."

"So why don't we do something about that? We'll get married, move into that house, find new jobs, and start our lives on new paths…together."

It all sounded too good to be true.

"I can't just leave the shop. I mean, Jackie's running it but she still needs my help."

"Are you kidding me? She's been kicking ass while she's been in charge. Have you seen the profit margins this month?"

I scratched the back of my neck. "I have." It couldn't be denied; Jackie was a natural in the shop. She'd bonded with the workers, managed the bills, introduced new drinks, and baked goods she and Tina made. She'd put up some new décor to freshen up the joint. Jackie seemed to be legitimately happy to be behind the counter.

"Her kids are in middle school now," Sam said. "They don't need her at home as much. She told Sandy she's loving being able to be out of the house. She was so bored at home waiting for everyone to come home," Sam said. "Jackie feels like she has a purpose now, Finn. She needs that place. She wants it."

I smiled, realizing she was right. I'd never seen my sister as happy as I had in these last few months. "So you actually think she'd live without me?"

Sam beamed.

"I do."

"Then 'I do,' too," I said, slipping the ring I'd been holding onto my left finger.

Her eyes welled up with emotion as she leaped into my arms.

"Really?" she asked, as though afraid I'd take my answer back.

"Really." I lowered my lips onto hers in such a way as to leave no doubts about my intentions. She shocked me when she pushed me away.

"Can we finally have sex now?" she panted.

I shook my head vehemently. "No."

"No?"

I gave her a soft kiss on the nose. "No to sex. But we *can* make love."

And that's exactly what we did. Many, many, times.

 Epilogue

We were engaged for almost a year before we held a November wedding. It was a simple affair at the courthouse. Jackie and her family were there to act as the witnesses as well as Joe and Maggie, who insisted on standing beside me. He wanted to be there in my dad's place. Although he still had trouble with some words due to the slight paralysis on the right side of his face, it was clear what he meant. He was proud of me and the man I'd become. It was enough to make the whole room cry.

Jackie insisted on a party back at the shop. The gang was all there. Sandy, who caught the bouquet; Rebecca, who emerged from her college essay application writing cave to be with us; Greg, who brought his mom; Kenny and his boyfriend; even Tina and her daughter, were all there with us. The boys from the bar even stopped in for some free cake, too. It couldn't have been more perfect.

I'd like to say we went somewhere romantic like Hawaii or Scotland, but we stayed at home, making love and gazing longingly into each other's eyes.

We had moved into our rental house the week after our engagement. That was a fun day. When moving day finally came, there was a foot of snow to deal with. No joke. The truck got stuck in the driveway, so we had to rent it a few days longer than planned until we could get it out. On the plus side, it was a first for both of us to make love in the back of a moving truck, so we called that day a win.

In the end, Sam was right. The house was perfect despite the obvious repair work that needed to be done in some areas. A new coat of paint and a few replacement windows and she'd be good as new. Most of the things were cosmetic. The bones of the house were rock-solid, just like our relationship felt.

The music store I was opening where the abandoned tanning shop on High Street used to be was gearing up to open later this year. I planned on selling guitar picks of every damn color there. Not just the pink ones.

For too many years, I'd put my love of music on the back burner. It had been my passion, my calling, once upon a time, but I'd ignored. No more. Sam had taught me to go after what you wanted with a bullheaded vengeance. After all this time, I was finally ready to open a store that sold sheet music and instruments, and I would give lessons.

Sam was busy working on her real estate license. Her undergrad was in architecture, but she had started classes on interior design but never ended up finishing in order to appease Ben, who wanted her home. She's been able to use those skills in staging open houses, though. Oh, the plans she has for our house! There are swatches all over the living room. I keep telling her she needs to go hit up our local movie star Morgan Malone. Her mansion could use Sam's touch. She laughed me off, but I could tell she was considering it. Heaven help Morgan if she decided to do it. What Sam wanted, Sam got. I should know.

Last spring Ben's ashes were buried along with a young maple sapling beside our house. The owner was honored with the request for him to spend his afterlife looking over Bucksville from his spot on the hill. Sam was crying that day, but they were tears of joy. She had her closure and felt calm that he was still so close to her.

In our spare time, Jackie and I were working on bringing back the Open Mic nights at the coffee shop, too. We'd cross promote each other there. Coffee and music made good dance partners. As did my wife and I. My wife. The words still made me smile.

Life with Sam felt like home. There was no other way to describe it. I didn't realize the vacancy that existed in my heart until she came in and showed me everything I was missing.

Sam and I still stop by Must Love Coffee every morning without fail. We share one of Jackie's homemade pastries, and I order myself an extra-large latte and Sam's medium Caramel Macchiato.

My favorite part of the day was when I got to kiss off the foam topping that always ended up on her upper lip. Then again, I suspected she did that on purpose, craving the kiss as much as I did.

"You know, you could order a Caramel Macchiato yourself," Sam chided me after such a kiss. "You sure seem to love it."

"I could, but then I don't get to taste you, too." I winked.

She laughed. "You must love coffee if you want the foam off my nose!"

I took her hand. "I *do* love coffee, Mrs. Allen. But I love *you* more."

And with that, I pulled her in for a very inappropriate public display of affection.

Danielle Bannister

Hug An Author

Wanna know how to hug an author (in the non-creepy way?) Leave a review, tag the author on social media letting them know you enjoyed their work, or tell your friends about their work. Any one of these things helps the author's work get seen by a larger audience, and that makes the author feel warm and fuzzy. Just like a hug.

You can follow **Danielle Bannister** in the following places.

Facebook: https://www.facebook.com/BannisterBooks/

Twitter: https://twitter.com/dbannisterbooks

Website: https://daniellebannister.wordpress.com/

Pinterest: https://www.pinterest.com/bannisterbooks/pins/

Newsletter: http://eepurl.com/bNvK7D

Amazon: http://bit.ly/DanielleBannister

Author Bio

Danielle Bannister lives with her two children in Midcoast Maine. She holds a BA in Theatre from the University of Southern Maine and her master's degree in Literary Education from the University of Orono. She has written the new adult thriller, *Enigma*, *The Twin Flame Trilogy: Pulled*, *Pulled Back*, and *Pulled Back Again*, as well as the Snarky Romantic Comedy: *The ABC's of Dee* and the light-hearted romance, *Doppelganger* and most recently the fantasy novel, *Netherworld* with co-author, Amy Miles. In November she'll join the *Havenwood Falls* series with her tale of ghosts. She has a collection of short stories called: *Short Shorts*. In addition, her work can also be found in the following anthologies: *2012 Goose River Anthology*, *2012 Writeous Anthology, 2013 Maine Writes: Maine National Writing Project Anthology*; and, *2013 The Stroke of Midnight: A Supernatural New Year's Anthology.*

How do you take your romance? Light or dark?

The Twin Flames Trilogy:

Pulled, Pulled Back, and Pulled Back Again

Enigma

Netherworld

The ABC's of Dee

Short Shorts

Doppelganger

Sneak Peek at Doppelganger

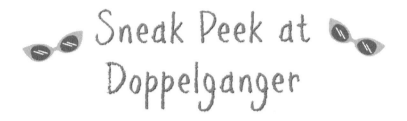

Chapter 1

I was not having a mid-life crisis no matter what my friends might have said when they found out I'd left. The decision to pack up and leave everything behind wasn't irrational. It was going to be the most logical thing I had ever done, in theory.

Everyone has a breaking point, and I had reached mine. Enough was enough. I was done. Done with the commute...done with the smog...done with the crowds. Done with fake people and the even faker tits that basked in the LA sun and I was most definitely done with my former boyfriend, Anthony, and his perfect wife getting pregnant with kid number three.

There it was; the straw that broke the camel's back.

So, I left. It felt good, too. For once in my life, I was taking charge of my own destiny. At least, that's what I kept telling my mother's voice each time she popped into my head during the twenty-three hour drive across the country.

Julie, honey, what are you running from?

Really bad choices, Ma.

When are you going to settle down and make me some grandbabies?

Um, never.

Maybe you could go back to school and finish your degree this time? It's so hard to explain to people what it is you do.

Tell them I work in an office. I'm a temp. It's not that hard.

Why don't you move back home? I heard Daniel Howards got divorced.

Thanks, Ma, I'll pass.

Those are the types of questions my mother would ask if I called—which is precisely why I didn't when I left. I chose to avoid the lectures and reminders that I had failed in life, yet again. I just wanted out.

My mother, of course, had no idea about my affair with Anthony. If she had discovered that I was the *other woman* she would have gotten down on bended knee and prayed for my soul, even though she hadn't been to church in years. The fact that her daughter had been sleeping around with a married man for the last three years, however, might be enough to send her back.

I'd send her a text whenever I landed someplace. When it was too late for her to talk me out of it.

The plan had been to end in Maine, the literal farthest away I could get from LA, but I ended up pulling over somewhere in New Hampshire to ask directions from a woman who was putting up a For Rent sign in her yard. We started chatting, and I decided, on the spot, I needed to live in *that* house.

New Hampshire was just as a good a state as any, as far as I was concerned. Now all that was left to do was unpack. Not that I'd brought much. Only as much stuff that fit in the rented SUV. The rest, I'd left behind, along with a note to my landlord letting him know not to expect a renewal of my lease. But before I began unloading the car to officially start my new life, I needed wine. And maybe some Doritos. Okay, and some ice cream too.

Thanks to the GPS in the SUV, I found the center of town...if you could call it that, and I pulled into the lot of the most Mayberry-looking grocery store anyone could possibly imagine.

"It's gotta have wine...even Andy Griffith needed to get drunk now and then."

I found my way inside and winced at the slight jingle noise the door made as I entered.

"Wow." That was the only word I could come up with for a store as tiny as this. It had five aisles total and not one dedicated for booze. This might be a problem. It was a far cry from the Big Saver stores I was accustomed to.

I grabbed one of the few carts by the door and started the hunt. Mercifully, the end of the first aisle had a small selection of alcoholic choices. I grabbed the biggest bottle of red wine they had and placed it into my cart where it rolled around precariously, as though drunk on its own existence.

One essential down. The chips proved to be a bit harder to find. I frowned. Nothing was where it should be. *Why were food stores all so different?* Couldn't they have a meeting or something and all agree on the same basic layout? No, instead, I had to waste my barely viable years searching for panty liners, olives, and makeup to cover up the zit growing on my forehead. Apparently, that defined life in your forties: leakage, sodium cravings, and acne. Honestly, when was the zit thing going to end? Sure, I'd been under a lot of stress lately, but was it really necessary to give me a third eye too?

Annoyed, I shoved the cart forward and began rolling my shoulders in small circles to ease some of the tension lodged there from the long hours behind the wheel. I'd never driven so long in such a short time and had no intention of doing it again. Not that I could, even if I wanted to. My funds were all but dried up.

I had saved some money by sleeping in my car at night instead of staying in a hotel, leaving me with about two hundred bucks to my name. I tried not to feel guilty about putting in a second bag of chips. I'd earned those.

As I rounded the corner in search of ice cream, I almost crashed, head on, into another cart. My wine rolled to the end of its metal cage and gave off a cringe-worthy *thunk* but, thankfully, remained intact.

"Oh, I'm sorry," the lady pushing the offending cart said. I glared at her for almost murdering my wine while I sized her up. She was about my age, maybe a few years younger, with a pudgy toddler in the front of her cart grabbing at everything within his sticky grasp. I tried not to gag at the crusty boogers lining the edge of his nose. I shivered. Kids were so gross.

"It's okay," I mumbled, trying to weave my cart around her.

The woman's smile abruptly faded. Likely because she realized I was an *out-of-towner*. Her eyes grew wide, and she took a step back. She gaped at me as though trying to form a sentence. Engaging in small talk with the locals was not high on my agenda, so I whipped around to the next aisle and came face to face with a line of purple and green plastic packages. *Oh, pads. Excellent.* One step closer to leaving this joint and drowning myself in wine.

When I placed the liners in my cart, I couldn't shake the feeling I was being watched, so I turned to glance behind me and saw the same woman sneaking a peek at me through an endcap of beef jerky before she dashed away.

"Okay…" Clearly, these small town folks didn't like strangers in their midst.

Opting to pass up the hunt for mint chocolate chip ice cream just to get the hell out of Dodge, I made my way toward the sole checkout person. Sole. As in…they only had one register. Not just one lane open. One lane total. Maybe moving to New Hampshire wasn't such a good idea.

I let out a breath and got in line behind a man in his seventies getting a shit-ton of cat food. Each can rang up *by hand.*

Oh. My. God. *I'm going to die waiting for this man to get his month's supply of cat food.*

Then again, maybe this was what life in a small town would teach me: to slow down, smell the roses and all that jazz. I mean, it wasn't as if I were late for anything. I had no job, and no one was waiting for me back at the rental. So why lose my cool over the change of pace? *Embrace it, Jules. The wine will still taste as sweet an hour from now.*

The towers of tuna slowly disseminated, exposing a sliver of the black conveyor belt, so I started to put my own items down.

"Looks like Hansel and Gretel prefer the flaked salmon," the woman at the register was saying as she plucked at the keys.

"Oh, they love it, Penny," the man said. "Hansel will try and get Gretel's before she's even done. I have to separate them when they eat."

The woman nodded sagely. "I have to do that with my three too," she said, bagging the cans in one of the cloth bags he had brought. "Oh, and you got one of those Lean Cuisines. You on a diet, Frank?"

My eyes widened in horror. Was this woman going to talk to me about my purchases as well? Would she seriously ask me if my panty liners really *were* super absorbent? Or if that liter and a half bottle of wine was just for me? Doesn't she know the Cashier Code? *Ask the customers if they found everything and how they want their items bagged. That's it. Take their money and move on. Do not engage. Do. Not. Engage.*

I began to panic about what I was going to say to her when I noticed the old man handed her a few bills. Actual paper money. Did this joint even have a credit card machine?

I looked around and didn't see any signs of one. *Oh, hell.* I was screwed.

Digging into my purse, I fished around in my wallet and, luckily, found a few twenties I had shoved in there before I left LA. The cash was all I had left from the sale of my *promise* ring; the one Anthony had given me. The ring that meant absolutely nothing in the end.

The cashier said her goodbyes to the cat man before she looked up at me with that same stranger-danger stare the lady with the snotty-nosed kid had given me.

"Do I know you?" she asked, slowly taking my liners and pulling them closer to the register.

"I highly doubt it," I said, reaching into my purse, this time to find my sunglasses.

She continued to bag the groceries with a watchful eye.

"Not from around these parts?"

"Nope."

"It's a little early for the foliage to bloom. Most tourists come by next month."

"Foliage? I could care less about leave color," I said.

She nodded slowly. "So, just passing through, then?" she fished.

"Look, can I just pay for my food and go?"

She gawked up at me, clearly offended, but sped up, nonetheless.

"You got an ID for the wine?" Her cheery tone had left.

I lowered my glasses and blinked at her. "I'm forty-two."

She pursed her lips. "And as soon as you show me that ID, you can have the wine."

So much for small town charm. I sighed and dug back into my purse for my ID but couldn't find it.

"Shit. It must have fallen out it in the car."

"Mmhmm," she said, sliding the wine aside, away from my bags. *This chick was actually confiscating my wine!*

Behind me, sticky-kid-lady started to unload her items. She and the cashier exchanged a few glances, probably making fun of me in their small town hick code way. I turned to glare at the mom. I saw her pointing at something behind me. She froze when she caught me looking at her.

"What?" I asked them. Neither woman said anything, but the cashier bagged the bottle of wine.

"No charge, dear. You have yourself a good day. New Hampshire welcomes you back." She smiled at me.

Confused, I snatched the bags and started to leave the store, pausing only when I spotted the object of their attention. It was nothing more that a large display of cheesy tabloids. I frowned and was about to turn away when I noticed something.

"What the hell?" I whispered, yanking my sunglasses off.

On the cover of every single magazine was a picture of a woman who looked *exactly* like me.

Continue the story online or in print.